Adva:

Going W

MW00413777

"Judith Day's *Going Where They Belong* (Wordrunner Press) is a book of gentle kindnesses....Told with a simplicity of language that expresses complexity of character, these stories place you squarely inside the quiet calamities of ordinary beings....these stories inhabit you with their specific and wonderful detail, their wit, their compassion."

—Linda Saldaña, review in *Eclectica*

"Day creates sentences that are so natural, so fluid, it is as if she is not writing them, but rather releasing them, like butterflies. These nine stories—filled with characters of longing, of love, of possibility, of acceptance (but without pat or hackneyed conclusions)—come to life in the light of her incandescent prose. *Going Where They Belong* is a chrysalis-bursting book that demands to be read. It is impossible to put down. It is a marvel."

—Erik Harper Klass, Author of
Polish Poets in Beds with Girls, and Other True Stories

"The nine stories in Judith Day's *Going Where They Belong* portray not quite ordinary people who are traveling, if not always literally, then emotionally, toward where they might belong, or where their wounds might be healed....In this engaging collection, you can read about a cabbie with a heart of gold who is exactly where he belongs or a disturbed woman who unintentionally murders an annoying acquaintance and now hasn't a clue where she is going. It's a gemlike, small collection I know I'll read again."

—Jo-Anne Rosen, author of
What They Don't Know: Selected Fiction

"A vibrant tapestry of tales....A wild and exhilarating ride with people who are brazenly themselves."

—*International Review of Books*

Praise for *Glowing in the Dark, Stories of Wounded Healers*

"Judith writes with skill, artistry and honesty, unfolding these complex, creative and sometimes troubling stories of humanity with lessons for all."

> —Jack Kornfield, author of *A Path With Heart*

"Beautiful and wise, *Glowing in the Dark* offers a triptych of compelling and complex psychological dramas. Judith Day writes with sorely-needed empathy, in prose graceful and precise. Her characters reveal lives that are heartbreaking, brutal, erotic, and ultimately affirming. A late debut, but well worth the wait!"

> —John Henry Fleming, author of *Songs for the Deaf* and Professor of Creative Writing at the University of South Florida

"Day's stories are always surprising and can be uncomfortable. They make you want to talk back. They will also make you want to read them again, to glean the knowledge between the lines."

> —Margaret Diehl, author of *The Boy on the Green Bicycle*

"Her characters, like the author herself, are unflinching in their pursuit of truth and beauty, love and meaning....It's a beautiful book and I'm already looking forward to her next."

> —Daniel Coshnear, author of *Separation Anxiety*

"*Glowing in the Dark* is the perfect title for this collection of stories, which are deep, clear-eyed visions of our interconnected souls' dark places as well as their light ones. The compassion glows. The prose glows."

> —Arlene Bernstein, psychotherapist and author of *Growing Season: Life Lessons from the Garden*

GOING WHERE THEY BELONG

stories

Dear Maria,

More of the stories you have helped me nourish over many years.

Love,
Ju

JUDITH DAY

Going Where They Belong

Printed in the United States of America

First Printing, 2024

Cover and book design by Asya Blue Design
Cover art: Mixed Media Collage by Barry Leibman
Author photo by Doug Wheatley

ISBN 978-1-9410666-3-8
Library of Congress Control Number: 2023946557

Wordrunner Press
Petaluma, California
www.wordrunner.com

TABLE OF CONTENTS

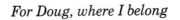

For Doug, where I belong

CABBIE

In Tony's business you never knew where you would end up, and a discount store might be near or far. But he knew where they were, and he went. He couldn't help himself. This morning at nine-forty-five, he pulled into the parking lot of the Pic "N" Save on Christy Boulevard. His niece had gotten a new kitten for Christmas, and she might need a bed for it. He had seen some the week before at the Pic "N" Save on Lemay Ferry, but when he got to the one on Christy Boulevard he looked all over, and they didn't have them. He walked around the store again, wanting them to be there.

But he saw a lot of other things he might buy. There was a toiletry kit that opened out and could hang on a bar. Tony was thinking about taking a trip sometime and that would be good to have. But he didn't get it. He also didn't get a tuna press, which squeezes the liquid out of a can of tuna without messing your hands. He passed up a tire inflator that works off your cigarette lighter, which he already had but thought he could use another one, and a hair clipper, which he had two of. He spent a moment browsing over the shoes, which he never bought because he never wore anything but his cowboy boots. They made noise on the linoleum. He didn't like the attention, but he liked the boots.

Walking past a mirror, Tony checked himself out. *Who's that handsome forty-some in the midnight blue tux?* That was a joke. Laclede Cab dress code in 1978 was black pants and white shirt, and black jacket in the winter. His face was pasty white and pockmarked, his eyes were small, and he had a serious underbite. Tony could see his belly puffing the jacket out. But he still liked seeing how he looked walking. His legs were short, but he had a stride.

A shopping cart loaded with a large box appeared from around a corner and stopped in front of him, blocking his way. It started moving again, and Tony stepped around it and found himself face to face with a man wearing a porkpie hat. He was Tony's height but older, his forehead creased and moist, a stubble of white beard glistening on his pale skin. His mottled hands gripped the cart as he struggled to make the turn without running into Tony. His eyes scanned the shelves. He stopped again, his back to Tony, and said something to himself, then moved on.

The half hour he allotted was up. On his way to the front door he paused over an ice cream scoop, walked away and walked back to it twice before picking it up, but then set it down on a pile of yoga mats halfway up to the registers. He finally left the store empty-handed. He had to squeeze past the old guy who was just starting to check out with his large box and a few other items, including the cigarette lighter tire inflator.

All day long he took in cash. The first sixty he folded up and put in his left boot. That paid the rent for the cab plus gas. After that, he should have been putting away for other things. He should have little pockets lining his boots, with labels: Rent, Food, Phone Bill, Electric Bill, Gas Bill, Truck Payment. But he didn't have those pockets and he was driving all over town with lots of cash, seeing department stores, consignment shops, Goodwill, Venture, Zayre's, EJ Korvette. Little unknown neighborhood shops. Central Hardware. Pipes and cigars, and he didn't smoke. Head shops, and he didn't smoke that either. Knicky-knacky shops. Grandpa Pidgeon's when he got out to St. Charles Rock Road.

He liked wandering around in all these different stores. He didn't always buy something. Just looking was satisfying. But buying something to have and take home was better, and usually he did. He carried the treasure away in a bag and stowed it in the cab's trunk. All the rest of the day he would think about it off and on. After work he took it home and unwrapped it, set it on the table or shook it out and draped it across a chair. He tried it on or put things in it or made a place for it on the counter or rearranged furniture for it or put it in a drawer or hung it in the closet.

He had started driving the cab four years before. After his first month on the job, he saw that even when he didn't spend money in the stores, he was spending what money is: time. Time is money, for a cabdriver. So last year Tony decided to limit his shopping to once a day, for half an hour, often at Dollar General or Family Dollar. Sometimes he went to one of the big discount stores, or Woolworths, or Famous-Barr's bargain basement. Last week he got a new mini-cooler one day, then a car cupholder, a pair of kneepads, a gallon of exterior flat white paint, and a dark red satin necktie. He didn't wear ties, but you never knew when you might need one.

As he did every weekday, Tony had picked up the cab at five this morning. The Ford Custom 500 was only six years old, but the shiny red paint was fading in a few spots on the hood and top. Inside, the black vinyl upholstery in the front seats was cracked in two places. The fabric headliner was sagging above the front seat. Over the driver's side there was a long tuck where they had glued it up, but on the passenger side it waved gently when the windows were open. Somebody else drove the car at night, and by the time it was turned over to Tony, any change that had fallen out of someone's pocket was already in the pockets of the garage guys who cleaned the cars inside and out between shifts. He checked the backseats anyway. He made sure the floor mats were in place and the inside of the doors were wiped down. Then he got in behind the wheel and pulled the seat forward. He turned on the engine, checked the gas, turned on the heat, and set the dispatch radio to Channel One. He eased out the driveway and drove a block to a Kwik Shop, got his coffee with cream and sugar, and drove another ten blocks to sit at Number Four to wait for the usual dispatch out to the lady and kid's apartment.

Number Four was on a side street, and this morning, snow was floating down, making it even quieter than usual. He left the engine on to run the heater and settled into the seat, sitting comfortable but straight, and started to sing "The Barber of Seville": *"Ecco ridente in cielo, spunta la bella aurora."* He sang it quietly at first, then loud, then slow and slower and then fast, sometimes getting completely silly with it because who cared? He never sang where anyone could hear him. When he stopped, he opened the windows wide. Even with full defrost on, the singing made the cab steamy. He gulped coffee.

Right on schedule, Dispatch came on the radio: "Four."

Tony switched on his microphone and answered, "Two-oh-eight, four." His cab's number was two-oh-eight, and he was sitting at the Number Four stand.

"Go get 'em, Tony," said Dispatch. It was the same call every day, so Dispatch didn't bother to tell him any more than that.

Tony cruised around the corner and pulled up in front of an apartment building where the lady and her daughter were waiting inside the glass door. He hopped out and went around to the passenger-side back door. As the mother and child came down the walk, Tony thought how big the girl was getting. Her hair looked cute in cornrows falling out from under her fuzzy white hat. When he had first picked them up, four years ago, it was a baby the mom carried.

He and the woman nodded hello as he held the door open for them. He drove them around the corner and down a block and around the next corner to another apartment building. He jumped out to trot around and open the door again. She paid the two bucks fifty, no tip. "Thank you," she said, and Tony said, "You're welcome." She walked the girl up to a door where another lady was waiting, and then she herself walked away: to a bus stop, Tony was sure, to go to work. The child was too precious to risk walking her to the babysitter's in the dark in that neighborhood, not the worst place in St. Louis but not the best either. But she couldn't afford any more taxi than that, so she walked herself off to the bus.

No other driver but Tony would have been caught dead at Number Four at five-thirty, because who wanted a two-fifty no-tip fare to start the day? Tony had fallen into it when he was new four years before, and he had come back every morning since. If you asked him why, he would say it was because somebody needed to do it and he didn't mind. That's what he told Dispatch: "I don't mind."

After that, he could go anywhere. This morning he drove over to Number Eight and struck gold, a couple going to the airport. They were talking about grandchildren misbehaving. At the airport he picked up a businessman going downtown who opened his briefcase and started writing something.

From downtown Tony picked up a dispatch and drove a lady home from her night job cleaning offices and then took an older lady to the doctor, where he parked the cab and walked her into the office on his arm. He got a dispatch for a teenager going to a piano lesson, which brought him to South St. Louis at nine o'clock. He went to a Steak 'n Shake for breakfast, bought a paper at a machine outside, and sat in a booth.

He ordered French toast and bacon and read about the latest war and accidents. He read about the Rams game he had seen on TV the night before. He read the obits. It was never anybody he knew but why not check? He read *Beetle Bailey*, *Little Orphan Annie*, and the *Family Circus* as he finished his coffee. Toward the end he was starting to get eager about where he was going after the restaurant. Still, he didn't hurry. Taking his time was part of the pleasure. Pic "N" Save was waiting for him.

Now the fun was over, and the rest of the day lay ahead. He got some more fares and a quick lunch, and early in the afternoon he pulled into Sixteen behind one other Laclede and two County cabs. Sixteen was worth waiting your turn because you usually got either a package pickup going out to West County or else an airport call from one of the hotels.

"*Some enchanted evening, you will see a stranger.*" He sang as loud as he wanted because across the street, three men were tearing up the pavement with a jackhammer. He felt sorry for those guys, out there on a freezing day. He had worked construction right after high school. It was hard, boring labor, and after work all the guys went to the foreman's house and drank beer. One night Tony suggested they put together a softball team and he nearly got jeered out of the room. They wanted to drink, not exercise. He gained thirty pounds, in muscle from the job and in his gut from the beer. He hated getting up every day. So he was glad when he turned twenty-one

9

and his cousin on The Hill got him a job tending bar. It was a classy place with lots of different people, and they paid him to not drink. He kept that job for sixteen years.

Working from 6:00 pm until two in the morning, he had his days free. There wasn't anything to do, so he started going to the malls or downtown, or even just to a Walgreens. Weekend days he hit garage sales. He furnished and refurnished his little apartment and crammed the closets with clothes and the back closed-in porch with tools and junk and got stuff for his mother and sister.

Just before heading to work in those days, Tony would go to Forest Park. There was a hillside with cottonwood trees, off the beaten track, where he strolled around and sang the songs he liked: opera, country, old torch songs, even nursery rhymes. He also made up a lot of songs. In good weather he would lie on his back watching the sunlight and shadows moving in the branches and leaves, alive in the wind. Everything was quiet except for their swooshing in the gusts.

When Tony was thirty-four, he met a girl at his sister's house on the Fourth of July. He was giving his niece piggyback rides around the yard, and there was a little boy who wanted one. The kid's mom stood there laughing and said it was okay and while he was playing with the boy, the mom went off and got Tony a hamburger and fixed a plate for him with slaw and potato salad. He ate it and she said, "Want some apple crisp?" Okay, he said. She was short with white legs and a gap in her front teeth. She moved around doing stuff with her eyes down, like mothers do. Her hair was puffed up and looked like she had put it that way especially for the party. Tony could picture her with it hanging down more normal.

Pretty soon he was living at her place. Patty had everything they needed, so he had a giant garage sale. She helped him put masking tape prices on almost everything he owned. People fought for parking places, and he joked with them and gave things away for less than asking price. A bony middle-aged woman took off happily with his wood-handled eggbeater, and a couple from Japan chatted incomprehensibly as they decided on his entire set of dishes and flatware. The only things he kept besides clothes and tools were his tape collection and his teak entertainment center, which replaced her dinky tape player.

In those days, he sang all the time, with the music playing or without it. Patty and Joey, who was three years old when they met, both liked Tony's singing. For nearly two years he hardly went into a store except to get groceries or buy something necessary for the house or something special for a birthday or Christmas. But after a while he and Patty started to argue. She seemed to want something from him, and he couldn't figure out what it was. Patty wanted them to talk when that's what they were doing. She wanted to move to the suburbs to have better schools for Joey, who wasn't even in school yet. She wanted them to go places. Tony started leaving earlier for work and driving out of his way to go to the malls. He had long since stopped his walks in the park.

It was springtime when Tony moved out. In a burst of yard sales and thrift shop visits, he furnished his new apartment within a week. He missed Patty and Joey terribly. In the summer he went to Joey's T-ball games, but in the fall the boy got busy with karate and school. In October, in the toy aisle at Venture, Tony couldn't decide on the right Christmas presents. He didn't know what Joey already had or wanted. By the New Year he had stopped calling and going over.

A couple of years later his job ended when the bar closed. He thought he'd like to do something different. Driving a cab would let him be outside, see the sights, and make his own hours. If he liked it, he might buy his own taxi sometime. As in the bar, he would get to meet a lot of different people and be with them for only short periods of time.

Sitting there at Sixteen thinking about it all, he started wondering about his life. Patty was probably right. The night they decided to break up, she had said, "Tony, you're just not going anywhere." Well, where *was* he going?

Just then Dispatch came on and told him. "Sixteen."

"Two-oh-eight, Sixteen," said Tony.

"Got a lady at 2213 Angelica. Says she's leaving town."

That was in the North St. Louis ghetto; people in that neighborhood generally used Metro Cab or Allen Cab. "For the airport?"

Dispatch laughed. "Not likely. She wants the bus station."

"Okay," Tony said.

"Fly me to the moon and let me play among the stars." He pulled up in front of a brick two-story with boards over a few windows. A lady ran out the front door and

13

waved at him. "The alley!" she called in a sort of whisper, pointing and waving to go around. *Right*, he thought. *I'm going into the alley in this neighborhood.* He hesitated until she came down to the cab. She was a thin little thing, color of pecans, moving quick, dressed in Capri pants, hiking boots, and a shiny silver jacket. Tony figured he would have seen tracks up her arms if it weren't for the long sleeves. Why she was in Capris in February he didn't know. They did have fake fur around the bottoms.

He rolled down the passenger-side window a crack, and she put one hand over the edge of it. Her nails were all bitten down, but they had fresh pink polish. She looked right at him, and she looked scared. "Can't you please pull around? I'm all ready to go." She glanced up and down the street. She didn't say it, but Tony knew she was leaving her old man, or her pimp. *Okay*, he thought. *I can help her out.*

He did a U-turn, and in a minute he was in the alley. She was coming down the stairs, the hiking boots feeling their way carefully because she was covered with clothes piled into her arms. He got out and opened the door, and she heaved them into the back seat and headed back up for more.

Waiting, meter running, Tony glanced up and down the alley and then looked at the clothes. They were flimsy polyesters, strong in the reds and purples. The woman returned, this time with paper grocery bags full of shoes and makeup and stuff. She went up the stairs for more. One of the bags fell over on the back seat, spilling a sparkly high heel and a red tennis shoe onto the floor. He stretched over and put them back in the bag and glanced around again. After two more trips she got into the front seat with two bags, and they took off.

"Where to?" he asked. He liked a flowery smell she brought into the cab with her. It reminded him of his sister's perfume.

First stop was the Civil Courts Building to check in with her probation officer. She was in there a long time, meter running. That's when he figured out this was going to be a freebie. There was no way she had the money to pay for this much taxi. What the hell.

She was smiling big when she came back, so Tony guessed the P.O. was as glad to see her leaving town as she was to be doing it. She scooted into the front seat, shoving aside a dirty cloth bag that said *Sierra Club* on it. The bag clanked with whatever was underneath hitting against the toaster crammed tightly on top.

"Where to?" he asked.

She looked at her life strewn around the cab. "I need some suitcases or something."

"How about Goodwill?"

Her smile at that moment was as fine as Tony had ever seen. He took off, blushing with pride and purpose, knowing better than any cabbie in the city where the nearest thrift store was.

The meter was astronomical by the time she got out of Goodwill with four old cases, three of them matching blue ones and the fourth a gigantic motley brown and yellow. She put two on the front seat and squashed herself with the other two into the back.

"Where to?" Looking over his shoulder, he saw the smile again.

"East St. Louis, the bus station."

Tony stared at her. That would have to be a good thirty minutes farther than the St. Louis Terminal at this time of day, and he didn't really know where it was over there.

"I know it's a drive. But I need to go to East St. Louis. Please." She was glancing around again, up and down the streets, and he understood: time to get out of Dodge.

When they pulled onto the bridge crossing the Mississippi, she settled down. The rustling and folding

16

got quieter and slower in the back seat. In the rearview mirror Tony saw her hold up a little mirror of her own and put on lipstick. She was sitting up very straight, holding her body still against the swaying of the cab and moving the lipstick carefully, paying serious attention in the way that Joey used to when he made stacks of blocks. Tony felt happy but also sad, like an old friend had come for a visit but was now packing up to leave.

It turned out she knew where the station was. While she went inside to buy a ticket, Tony checked the meter. He noticed that she had too. She came back and Tony carried some bags in for her. "It's two hundred twenty-seven dollars, but just give me whatever you can," Tony said. Mister Nice Guy.

She smiled one last time, all glistening teeth and shiny pink lips. "Thank you, Brother. I really thank you." She handed him five bills.

They were hundreds. He started fumbling for change, but she laughed. "No, no," and she turned away and moved on into the line pushing her cases and bags with her feet.

He looked again at the bills. He guessed her work paid well, but he hoped she didn't have to earn her money that way in her new life. Or, if it was her old man's stash she cleaned out before she took off, Tony was sure he deserved it. Before leaving he went up to her and said, "Lady, you take it easy now. Good luck."

Once in the cab, he tucked the five Ben Franklins into his boot and told himself they were in a pocket called Savings. He turned off the dispatch radio. The gray daylight was darkening as he drove out of East St. Louis, dodging potholes. Boarded-up storefronts were jammed together with neon-lit bars, dark churches, bright diners, and brighter corner stores. Harsh blue streetlights were coming on. Men hung out in small clusters and little boys chased each other down the sidewalks. Girls dressed in long fake fur coats and high heels stood in groups of two or three smoking cigarettes. He kept his eyes open for Dollar stores but didn't see any.

Driving over the bridge, he started singing the Eagles: *"Take it easy, take it easy, don't let the sound of your own wheels drive you crazy."* He dropped the melody line and sang it operatic style and then as a Gregorian chant. *"Li-i-igh-ten u-u-u-u-up while you sti-ill ca-a-a-a-a-an."* He treated himself to a steak dinner at Denny's.

The next morning it was the lady and little girl again, and then a few other calls until it was nine o'clock and he had breakfast at an IHOP. He read the paper: *Beetle Bailey, Dennis the Menace, Little Orphan Annie, Family Circus*. He scanned the obits and looked at his watch. He put his jacket on and left, planning his route to the Family Dollar on South Grand. He thought they should call it the Family Circus. It was certainly entertaining for him.

As he drove, he felt the eagerness just the same as any day, but he was also feeling tired. It was another gray morning, not yet snowing but he could smell it in the air. He thought of Tower Grove Park just down the street. The snow, when it came, would cling to the branches and frost the curving iron cupolas and pile silently onto the slats of benches. If he walked there, he would make footsteps on the paths. He could stop and look around at the whitening tree limbs, and look back at the smooth prints left by his cowboy boots.

He drove to the store. Then, even though everything seemed to be the same, something different happened:

when he got there he didn't stop. He felt the little excitement he always felt when he got close. He was going to pull off into the parking lot. But he didn't stop. He drove right by and kept on driving, no idea where he was going. He wanted to turn around and go back. But he didn't.

He ended up at Number Twelve and got in line behind two Black and White Cabs. The drivers were lounging on their fenders yakking it up, each of them spewing a little cloud of warm air in front of his mouth. Tony thought there should be words in the clouds like in the cartoons. Once in a while, one of them would take his hands out of his pockets and blow on his fingers.

Tony kept his windows rolled up and pulled his cap down and pretended to nap. Behind his eyes he saw passing images: the cabbies talking, the front door at the Family Dollar, the benches in the park down the street. Patty, curled up on the couch with some other guy. *"Avagabeela, zippideedoodah, bibbity bobbity boo,"* he sang under the cap. He took the cap off and straightened up in the seat. *"Put 'em together and what have you go-o-o-ot?"*

Dispatch put out a call and he headed north on Kingshighway to pick up a fare checking out of the Park Plaza Hotel going to the airport. It was an old man. He was shorter than Tony and was dressed up in a suit and vest. He carried a soft gray overcoat. His white hair was combed from one side over the bald top to the other side, and his chin had a wispy white beard. It started to snow as Tony loaded his bags into the trunk. "Careful," Tony said, indicating the curb, as he opened the back door for him, and off they went.

"What airline?" Tony asked.

"United," said the man. "Thanks." Then he said, "How's it going?"

"No problem, it's going good," Tony answered. "How about you?"

He laughed. "No problem, no problem. No problem for me, either."

They were quiet for a moment and then the man corrected himself. "Well, I said no problem, but the truth is I'm old and nobody loves me." His laugh was a crackling sound and then he hiccuped. Tony laughed with him but didn't know what to say. The man hiccupped again a few times and fumbled in his pocket and swallowed a pill.

They were stopped in traffic and the cab felt too quiet. Tony started out just humming, but right away the words came out on their own. "*Ecco ridente in cielo*," he sang. Very soft, like the air in the cab. "*Spunta la bella aurora*."

21

GOING WHERE THEY BELONG

"Bravo!" the man cheered him on. "Bravo, bravo, more!"

He only knew the one phrase, so he started it over. "*Ecco ridente...*" The same words over and over all the way out I-70, but he sang it in a lot of different ways. Pulling into the drop-off line at United, he finished up, sweet and gentle, to the tune of "Twinkle Twinkle Little Star," timing the end to the moment he stopped curbside.

The passenger sat in the cab blowing his nose while Tony got his bags from the trunk. It took the man a while to get out. Standing on the curb, he put his hand on Tony's arm but then pulled it away to get some bills out of his front pocket. "No change."

Tony put them in his pocket without looking at them and gave the man a quick, tight hug around his shoulders with one arm. "Thank you," they both said.

He drove around the circuit to the lower level outside baggage claim and got in line. It was always long, but it moved. He kept the engine on and inched forward every minute or two. He would see the lady and her kid the next morning, but other than that he never knew who would get in. He talked if they wanted that, or just listened, or no one talked and they cruised together in the quiet, feeling the smooth ride and seeing the city wheeling past, sitting together at the stoplights, watching the sun come up and the snow come down.

STUPID BUDDHA

That stupid Carol kept following me, shouting at me, calling me a bitch. "Give me a cigarette, you bitch." She finally pushed me and I pushed back and when she pushed again, I tripped backward over a root and slammed my backbone into a tree. It hurt like hell and I started screaming. I picked up a log and swung it at her head as hard as I could. She fell, and I kept hitting her and screaming. I hit her five or six times before I ran off. I could hardly run with that stupid skirt twisted around in my legs and I was killing my feet on the rocks because those damn shoes of hers I was wearing fell off my feet. I ran down to the water. I was heaving and moaning like a crazy person.

There was the tiniest bit of daylight still left in the sky, but everything was black all around except for some tree shapes. The river was purple, almost black. I heard the water rippling. I hated dark coming, but I liked the sound of the water. My breathing slowed down. When I get scared, I stop and breathe. In eighth grade, my Girl Scout leader told me I should do that, and I never forgot.

I went back, walking soft over the rocks on the outside soles of my feet. I found the shoes and put them on. They are these little flats with a bow on the top, hardly any help at all in the woods.

Then I went over to where Carol was. It was easy to tell she was dead. She was lying facedown, and her head was turned in a bad way. It was covered with blood, all in her hair, and I could see one eye was stuck open. I thought she might blink or move, but she didn't move at all. She was still under the log I dropped, and her skirt was up from her white legs. One arm was pulled up under her, and the other was sticking out like a broken branch hanging off a tree. She was wearing loafers and I thought about trading shoes, but I didn't want to touch her.

I took off walking, heading downstream. Now it's morning, and I'm damned tired after walking all night down this river. Some of the way has a trail but a lot of it doesn't. I must have slipped and fell a hundred times last night. My legs are all scratched up, and I hate this stupid tight skirt and these horrible little shoes she talked me into wearing that keep making me fall. My right leg is bleeding from the time I fell right out flat on my face and skinned my shin and anklebone. Tore open my shin, really. It's a gash I don't even want to look at. I hurt all over and I'm tired and hungry. I wish I had a cigarette. I'm so thirsty right now I could drink pig's blood. I wish I could drink the water here but that would be stupid with this river.

I should get away from the river, but it's at least a path. I passed the Tremble Road Bridge a while ago and could have gone out south, headed up into the hills or something. But I don't know what's up there. It just looks like trees and trees. I'd get lost in them, but I couldn't stay on the road because somebody might see me. So I'm going to stay on this damn river, but I do wish I had had the damn sense to head upstream instead of down, because I'm just going back toward all those people I've spent the last ten stupid years with. I'm way downstream now but I'm mad at myself that I headed down instead of up. There are too many towns down this way and the bay isn't that far, and then where will I go when there's no more river to follow? The worst thing is that I know all those people down this way, especially when I get down to Chambers Road and all. If I stay with the river, I'll have to pass through all those places. Jimmy's probably down there with his gang of fools. But I guess I'll have to do that unless I walk all the way back up and go right past dead Carol again. No way, José. They've found her by now for sure, people fishing early morning out at that Smiley's Beach.

I guess I'll stop for a rest. I'm going to sit on that big rock for a while. There's a brown or gray nothing bird on that little pine branch, singing like crazy. I think he has to shout like that, same thing over and over. Birds have to do it whether they want to or not. It's a lot of work.

He's stopped now. He's looking at me. I think he's hungry. If I had bread or popcorn, I'd give him some.

I hated that Carol. The whole world is better off without her, but she isn't, I guess. The world would be better off without me, too, but I'm still here. I'd say it was her fault she's dead. But it isn't really. It's my fault. When I was picking up that branch, which I could hardly lift but I did, I had a feeling I should stop. I knew it was going too far. But in a way I really couldn't stop; I really couldn't. But I know I should have.

I didn't want to kill her. I didn't feel like that at all. Sometimes, lots of times, I *do* want to kill somebody.

The first time was when I was little, and my mother was washing the dishes. She was mad and drunk and throwing the dishes around and talking nasty. She washed a big knife, and I thought of killing her with it. I was standing behind her, outside the screen door. Then I remember one time when I was in sixth grade the neighbors had kittens. I was petting one and I thought of strangling it. It would have been easy. But why would I do that? Little kitten never hurt anybody. Sometimes I like to kill bugs. When I kill mosquitoes, I'm glad. I used to squirt Raid around in the bathroom when I was in high school, and I was really glad the roaches were going to die. For a while I had a car, before I lost my job at the K-mart. When a squirrel would run into the road, I sort of wanted to hit it, but I'd put on the brakes or swerve around it instead. Little squirrel never hurt anybody.

Last night with Carol, I didn't feel that way at all. I didn't have any urge to kill her. I just wanted to get her away from me. She's coming at me, screaming. "Nobody asked you to come up here with me anyway," is what she said. And then she's coming at me again, yelling at me, "Give me a cig, you bitch. You crazy stupid bitch." I should have been Yosemite Sam and told her "Back off!" But she was drunk and on a tear. Then she pushed me.

29

It was too much, and I grabbed that log. I think she was asking for it, honestly. We were alone on a riverbank at night, and she went too far, and I went too far. Carol gets in fights all the time, but she hurts inside, too. She was a bitch, but I've also seen her cry sometimes. She was in a horrible tangle inside. I should have run away instead of hitting her, but I didn't feel like running away.

Now I am, though. All night long, going downstream, which I've decided I don't want to do. I think I might go back upstream after all. If I walk right by all those police and all, they won't think I did it. Or I could leave the river before I get to where Carol is, go up Lyman Cross Road to Salt Springs Road and up to Howardville. I could get breakfast there. I don't know anybody in Howardville. That sounds a lot better than going back where I've been for ten years. I will hate to go all the way back upstream when I just spent all last night going down. But going upstream in the daylight is bound to be better than downstream at night, even with that bright moon. Last night that moon kept shining on rocks and logs and trunks of trees, and sometimes I'd think it was Carol's body underneath, with her eye stuck open.

Thank god I had my flashlight. Ever since I was a kid it's been important to me to have a flashlight. I can wake up at night and shine my light around to get a bearing on the place, whatever place it is. This flashlight I have now is a small purse one on a keychain. Jimmy gave me a Buddha that I hung on the chain with it. It's not one of those fat Buddhas that's laughing that's supposed to be for good luck. This one isn't laughing. It just sits there with its hands folded in its lap. The top of its head is knobby and that's where the hole is that the chain goes through so you can carry it around. Jimmy said even if it's not laughing, it's bound to be lucky. I don't know. Most of what he told me is lies anyway. All this one does is help me get hold of the flashlight in the bottom of my bag. After last night walking down this river, I need new batteries. I'll get some when I get to Howardville. I hope Howardville has a Goodwill so I can get some jeans and sneakers. Goodwill always has good stuff.

Okay, then. I'm going back upstream. I have a place I'm going and things I need to do.

When I left my aunt's house to hitch into town yesterday it was already three-thirty, and I made sure I had all my important possessions in my bag because I didn't plan to go back. I have walked away from her house many times carrying everything I have in this bag because I thought of not going back, and a few times I did stay out overnight. But usually I go back even though it's not what I planned to do. There really isn't much of anyplace to go. One time Murphy Anderson saved his unemployment money and got a bus to the airport and then took an airplane all the way to Los Angeles. He planned to go to Hollywood and Beverly Hills and all, and Disneyland, but he told us he just stayed in the airport a few hours and then flew back and took the bus back to his house. He was gone overnight and nobody believed him, but he showed us the ticket receipts with his name on them.

When I hitched to town yesterday, I didn't go to Chambers Road because I'm so sick of those people. I decided to go up to the far end of town where I usually never go. I was in a little shopping center and about to drink a soda when Carol turns up, yelling my name. One of the last people in the world I wanted to see. I didn't say much and she jabbered away, in higher gear than usual even. She's loud and coarse. Her boobs jiggled in her tight white blouse, and she was leaning too close. Her makeup smelled. I have no idea what she was saying. She was being friendly. I didn't want her friendship but there she was. I've known her for a long time, and she thinks she's my friend because I'm nice to her and nobody likes her.

She was so excited she spilled my cup of soda all over my pants. I walked away from her, but she followed. It turns out she lives up at that end of town. She bothered me until I went with her to her room, to clean up from the soda, and that's when she made me borrow her skirt. I couldn't wear my sneakers with that, so I wore some of her old flats. I never should have left my clothes at her place.

I don't know why we ended up at Smiley's Beach. It was a stupid idea, her idea. She made me buy beer, and we hitched up there and watched the river for a while. Everybody else left. We should have, too. I should have, but I didn't plan to go back to my aunt's and where else would I go? I should have left, but I left too late. She was yelling. She had turned from friendly into mad and that was more than I could handle. She pushed me and I hit her.

Now I see her face all bloody. Her damned eye is open. Stop it!

I'm not going to think about that.

I'm starting to feel really angry again. I'm angry at Carol for probably ruining my life. I hate this damn heat and these stupid bugs and dirt around here. I hate her shoes and skirt most of all.

Goddammit. I just threw her asshole shoes in the water and then fished them out because I will need them until I get to the goddamn Goodwill. If there even is one up there in that stupid town, which I'll probably never get to anyway.

This stupid skirt hurts my waist, so I just pulled it off and I don't even care that I tore it. Goddamned skirt! Then I tore it more, on purpose, and shoved it in the dirt. I hate it. It's Carol's extra skirt that is all the wrong colors for me anyway and has too many big flowers. The button is gone, and every step I take, the zipper pokes me in the side.

I have my own T-shirt on, thank god. It's turquoise, my favorite color, and doesn't match the skirt at all, but I'm glad I have it. It's very funky now with sweat, but at least it's mine. I'll take it off.

My crotch is itching from wearing the same underpants too long. I'm taking them off too.

My face feels burned, from heat and dirt. My hair is hot. My head and neck are sweating. I might get a haircut in town, too, if they have a Supercuts for twelve dollars. But I should probably save that money because there is not that much money left. I could kill Carol for talking me into buying beer which she was the only one who drank.

I won't buy cigarettes in Howardville because I've decided to quit.

I think I'm going to get in the water to freshen up. This looks like a good place. This right here looks way better than Smiley's Beach. There's no fish smell or slime along the edge.

I'm feeling much better now. My poor feet needed the cold water. They're muddier now, but the blood from that bad cut is washed away. The sweat is gone from my whole body. Flies are bothering me, but they aren't too bad here. I will hate to put that skirt on again, and the shoes are horrible. But I feel a little better. The sun is coming through. I'm letting my clothes air out on branches. I washed my underpants even though I'll have to put them on wet. Or I could wear no panties for a while until they dry more.

I'll just sit here awhile. I think I'll just go through my bag. Here is my nail clipper and wallet. Here is my lipstick. Here are matches. Here is my foldup fan. Here is my toothbrush and my small travel toothpaste. Here is my flashlight. That Buddha on the other end of the chain won't even sit up. Jimmy gave me such a stupid Buddha. Those laughing ones usually sit up, I think. I saw one in a store, and it was sitting. This one looks like it's sitting with its legs crossed but it's too narrow to really sit. It's almost worthless, I would say.

Now I'm trying to make myself open the keychain to throw the Buddha away and I'm afraid. Jimmy said the thing would be good luck. There's really no need to throw it away except after last night I'm wondering if it's bad luck instead. But Jimmy gave it to me last winter and it hasn't been all bad luck since then, not any more than usual.

This Buddha has a hole in his head where the keychain goes through. I think he may have shot himself with a gun. If he lived through that, maybe he is good luck after all. Like Jesus lived through all his stuff.

I hear a car up ahead; I must be close to Lyman Cross Road. When I get there, I'll turn right and go to Salt Springs Road, turn left and walk up to Howardville. If someone talks about dead Carol, I'll look shocked. That's really terrible, I could say. I can tell them all about my family in Canyon City—I can say I have a father working in the mill. I can have a brother. He can have a wife and a new baby. I'll say how I stay home and go to the college over in Central City. I met a boy one time who did that, went to the college in Central City. He was learning music, I remember.

But now I'm afraid to go through with all these plans. I don't ever know what I should do. I think I shouldn't have come back up here, now that I'm almost back at the place where it happened. I just want to get past it and go on up the river like I planned, but I can't get myself to go.

This always happens to me. I don't ever know what I should do. So I'm going to sit here and breathe. A lot of days it is scary to go out, and that's what I'm feeling now. Sometimes I end up spending the whole day on my bed. One day when I was lying on my bed and doing the breathing, I got very peaceful. I had been thinking about things and was very confused and hated myself. I didn't see any way out of my troubles, out of the way my life is. I wasn't angry just then, but I hated myself. Then I remembered to breathe instead of think, and my stomach stopped hurting. For a while I couldn't do anything else but feel my breathing. The clock was humming next to my ear, and my aunt was cooking fried chicken in the kitchen. I sort of wanted to think but not enough to bother doing it. Breathing was just much better than thinking. I fell asleep finally, which is not something I do that often.

I don't know what to do. I can't sit here by this pool all day. So I'll just sit here and breathe now until I know what to do.

That was one thing about hitting Carol with that branch. I didn't have any doubt or confusion about it. It felt really good to not be confused and just do something. It was an accident she died, and I'm sorry if anybody asks me, but right now I think about that feeling of doing it and it makes me feel as peaceful as the breathing did that one time.

I think I'll brush my teeth. River water won't probably hurt for that.

Then I want to sleep for a while. I wonder if I can. I never can sleep but maybe I'd better sleep now. It's daytime so I don't need the flashlight but what I want is that Buddha. I'll just lie down here and hold this Buddha next to my stomach. It's not as good as a stuffed animal, but it's the closest thing. That helps me go to sleep sometimes. If I can't sleep, at least I'll just breathe for a while. And then I'll take myself on up the river, no matter what.

Up the river. Ha-ha. That's where they'll be sending me. It was self-defense, but they won't believe that.

I'm not going to think about all that.

Lying here on the grass I did the breathing, and after a while I noticed that this place is filled with bells. Over there are little white flowers shaped like bells. The moss around them looks like tiny green bells. Some bug is scratching its wings together and it rings like a bell, *ding-dong*.

A big ant just fell off a branch into the water. Fortunately there is hardly any current in this slow river so he didn't get pulled away. I scooped him out with a leaf, and he ran away fast when I put him on the ground. Now it's a funny thing: when I saw him fall in, I had that feeling I used to have with the mosquitoes and squirrels and the kitten, a kind of excitement and meanness. I liked seeing that ant get scared and twist himself all around and not be able to get out of it. I wanted him to die. But quick as a wink, not even thinking, I rescued him.

I hear some more cars at Lyman Cross Road. Their tires go across the gravel from right to left. They can't see me. I feel safe here, so I'll stay for a little while longer, but then I'm going to head out. I'm definitely going to keep on going upstream after all, no matter what. I don't know if it's the right thing, but that's what I'm going to do. There's nothing to do down where I used to be, and it makes me sick to think of seeing Jimmy again and all those same old places.

THE SUNDOWN SIDE
OF THE ROCK

"**B**illy, that's it!" My brother pokes his arm from the back seat and points straight ahead at the giant rock standing in the middle of the desert. He's been sleeping for hours, and I see in the rearview mirror that his eyes are dumb and his hair sticks out on top like a blond knife.

"Yeah, that's it, ain't it?" I say. We've been looking for the thing for a week, and I saw it about half an hour ago. The road is a straight dust track and the rock is the only thing there is to see, rising a couple hundred feet high out of the sagebrush. The desert is red and brown around here and the rock doesn't match. It's dark gray. As we get closer, I'm totally sure this is the one. I see the split partway up where one side is rounded off and

41

smooth and the other side is jagged and sharp. It was that jagged side where me and Dad climbed up.

Tom squeezes himself into the front, dragging his sneakers over the metal box taped between the seats. "Damn," he says as he leans back against the vinyl. It's hot and we don't have shirts on. His chest is striped with ridges from the blanket on the back seat.

I shove a box of Oreos across the dash. "Want a cookie?"

He sticks his head out the window to look all around at the sky. He's looking for the cloud we've been following, which is more or less how we get from one place to another. That's how Dad used to travel.

"It's gone," I say. "It dissolved. But it was right over here somewhere."

He sits back and says nothing.

I can tell he's remembered he's mad at me, so I say, "Tom-o, have a cookie."

"Thomas," he reminds me. Last week he decided he wants to be called Thomas, but I usually forget. He takes the last three Oreos in the box.

"Thomas," I say. Making peace, I hope.

I gear down as we get close. I've always remembered this place but I didn't exactly know how to get here. It was three years ago when we camped here with my dad. Tom was six, and I was thirteen. Back then Tom always sat in back and I rode shotgun. We drove up this same dirt road then in the same old Jeep Cherokee, and Dad said, "Hey, Billy, which side is sundown?" I pulled out my compass and told him to go around the right side of the rock to about one o'clock, one-thirty. That should line us up with sundown. We always camped on the sundown side of anything that was big enough to keep you in its shadow for quite a while when the sun came up. My dad didn't want to wake up too early because he said he was on vacation, which wasn't quite true. I didn't want to because I'm usually up most of the night, and when I fall asleep just before dawn, I like to stay asleep for a while. Tom was little and he liked to go along with what me and Dad wanted.

Driving up to the rock back then, Dad pushed his Dodgers cap back from down over his eyes. "Gonna be a good place, up there." He licked his lips and gave me a punch on my arm, smiling big with his mouth closed. He was skinny, and his knees flopped around some as he drove, especially when he'd been driving a long time. His feet were duck-toed on the pedals. I was learning to drive then and paid close attention to how you do it. He

43

dangled his arm out the window and banged on the door with his fingers, and sang, *"Oh, she jumped in bed and covered up her head and said I'd never find her! Da-da da da da, da-da da da da, so I jumped right in behind her!"* He always sang that.

I hum the same song now as I pull around and park right where he did. I turn off the engine. Like before, we are the only ones here. It's dead quiet except for insects. Tom jumps out and starts to unload the back. I sit for a minute looking at the steam coming out from under the hood. It wasn't even a climb but just the hot sun got it going. It's time to get rid of this Jeep. Dad used to trade cars a lot, but he kept this Jeep Cherokee for a long time. "One of the first SUVs ever made. V-8 juice." I like it, too.

But it's hell to sleep in. I've always been big for my age, but I'm probably too big to sleep in any car now. Before the Jeep, when I was about twelve, we had a green Falcon station wagon where me and Tom could lie in the back, and it was almost long enough for me. It felt good in there at night with my brother breathing right next to me. Dad slept across the front seat. Back before that, when I was about nine or ten, we had a Chevy El Camino. I asked Dad why he got so many old cars. He told me they weren't old and that he always bought something from the year he was born, 1974.

Tom's already got the cooler and sleeping bags hauled down the slope into a wash of willow trees to the same spot as before. He comes back to the Jeep and climbs on top and unties the chairs and hands them down to me. He carries them and I carry the box of pots and dishes and the box of food on top of that and we go back down the hill to the camp.

Not too many people must ever come here because it looks about the same to me. There are the stones ringed up for fire, some logs to lean on, and two big flat rocks for fixing food. Three years ago, Tom and I slept under a tree where somebody sometime had hung up a string mop, and the mop is still hanging there. I look at another tree and see the wooden bowl I fixed between some branches to give water to the birds.

We make the fire, and I start peeling potatoes and boiling a pot of water. I bring it up again. "You gotta go to school sometime."

Tom is breaking up dead sticks for more fire. "Nuh-uh."

"Yes, you do."

"Don't."

"Do."

45

"Don't either."

"Do you even remember school? It's fun. You can screw around with a lot of kids."

"I never went to school."

"Yes, you did." Once we stayed at Aunt Laurie's and Tom went to kindergarten. I got put into the fourth grade with kids a lot smaller than me. We left in early spring so neither of us finished.

"I know everything I need to know," he says. "I can read and write, better than you. I'm good at math. Dad taught me everything I need. There isn't any reason to go to school."

"You can't read better than me."

"I didn't say that. I said I write better."

We both laugh because it's true. And because he always wins the arguments.

Tom falls asleep before dark, and I pull my pouch out from my underwear and count the money. There's about enough left for a few more tanks of gas. Used to be when Dad got down that low, he got some work for a while. I can do that too. But Dad never saw gas get up to four bucks.

It was over a year ago that he didn't come back one day after he walked into town in Barstow, California.

46

He had been arrested before but always came back in three or four days. This time we waited a week and then I walked on into town, too. I asked around at the library, at a couple of town squares where guys hung around, in a Food4Less parking lot, and at two pool halls. I watched the county jail for a while. A lady and a boy about Tom's age came along and were going in, so I ran over and asked if they would keep an eye out for a tall, thin man with not much hair and a brown beard. They came out after a while and said they hadn't seen him in there. I worked the second half of that day at a fruit stand and then went and got bread and lunch meat and took it back to the county park where we were staying.

We waited a whole month. I went into town looking every few days. I moved the Jeep around to different parks, but there were only so many where we could stay for free. We'd been getting the eye from the park attendants, so we finally took off. It was a hard thing to do.

I never traded a car, but I'm going to look for a little station wagon. A Toyota or Honda, or a Subaru. From 1996, my year.

I sit in the fold-up chair a long time, thinking about girls. Last night we stayed at a hot springs in the middle of nowhere, where anybody who can find the place and

47

four-wheel up there goes in naked and relaxes with joints and beer. Dad used to go there. It's a good place to sell weed. I've been there a few times already this year.

Last night there was this girl there named Juniper. Her hair was as short as a boy's and spiked with frosty blue green, like pine needles. My dad likes girls' hair long and blond, but I don't mind it being short and green. Her neck was pale, so maybe she cut the hair just the other day. She was pale all over, though. Out of the water, she put a white shirt on.

Her and me wandered off from everybody and got into a lower pool. The sun was going down when we paddled around the edge of a big hot bubble to a place under a little cliff where there was a rock or two underneath the surface to stand on so you didn't have to tread water. She started asking about where I live and all. I said Oregon. But I didn't ask about her because I don't care about that and so she took the hint and got quiet too. Her face got red from the heat, but she stayed. We waved our arms around in the water and her boobs moved with the waves. I thought of saying things and maybe kissing her, but after a while I just took off. I swam back and went to check on Tom, who was still playing with some littler kids in the shallow part. I took him to get some food. A guy was grilling ears of corn and hot dogs outside his camper truck. I traded him some weed, and me and Tom ate real well. Another guy gave us two big soft tomatoes that we ate sitting right in the dirt. The juice ran all over us, so we had to get back in the pool to rinse off.

Then we went on to bed, but as usual I was awake forever. I kept on thinking about Juniper. I even thought of getting up and going to find her.

One time right before he left, Dad asked me about a girl who had followed me around at one of the campgrounds. We were in the Jeep the day after leaving there, and Tom was asleep. "So what'd you think of that girl?" he said.

I hadn't thought anything of her. "She was okay," I said. Dad was driving barefoot and that looked good to me, so I took off my shoes and socks too. "She asked me where I went to school," I said. People always did that. "I said Flagstaff." Then I told him I missed school and I asked him if he would get a house.

"Maybe," he said. "So you liked her?"

"Okay, some. Nothing special," I said, which was something he always said.

"Nothing special," he said. "That's the truth sometimes." After a few minutes he said, "But you know, Bill,

49

you're going to have to try that thing out sometime."
He gestured at my lap. "Hell, I was just a little older
than you when you were born. *Oh, she jumped in bed
da-da-da-da-da.*"

I was fourteen then. I keep thinking if I meet somebody now it might be different, but last night I just
walked away from Juniper.

Finally I lie down in my bag. It's dead quiet, but after
a while I hear a wind picking up out across the open
space. It's another while before the branches above us
start waving. The light sky between the branches is like
a moving lace curtain. Once or twice the handle on the
string mop clunks against the tree. Out on the horizon,
the moonlight is starting to shine. It glows around the
edges of the rock like a halo. The place Dad and me
climbed up is on the moon side. I could walk over there
right now, and it would be lit up so bright I could see well
enough to climb it again. But I'm not going to, tonight
or tomorrow either. I can do most things by myself, but
I wouldn't try that without him.

I sleep then and the next time I look the moon is
dead overhead and everything is all lit up. Even the Jeep,
which is blue, looks bright white in the moonlight. The
orange paint over the rusted places looks like strange

letters. The wind is really flying around us, the mop is banging like crazy, and the lace up above is a wild dance. I sit up and get hit dead-on by bugs and moths and dust, which is funny, so I laugh and lie back down.

But I don't sleep. A small cloud comes up, moving across the sky at a good clip. If it was morning and we were ready to drive, we'd start off chasing it. That's what Tom wants to do. He wants to go here and there and follow the clouds and not care where we end up, like we did with Dad.

I've tried following the clouds, but that turns out to be harder than I knew it was. But I know something Tom doesn't: Dad didn't really do it that way. He only said he did. Sometimes he did that for fun, but a lot of the time, he had some things in mind about where to go. And so do I. Yesterday's cloud just happened to bring us to the rock we were looking for, and I'm thinking there's a cloud coming up pretty soon that might end us up at Aunt Laurie's around the time that school starts for a nine-year-old. That will be just around the time of my seventeenth birthday, which is when they will let me into the Army. The Army might not be so bad. They teach you a job. I can do what somebody tells me to.

But Tom has to do things his own way. Last winter we

were stuck in an empty campground in heavy rains out at the coast, nothing to do for days but sleep. I woke up once and pushed my foot over to where Tom's leg was, but it wasn't there. I figured he was out peeing. But he didn't come back. I squinted out the steamed-up windows and saw that our big poncho was slung over the picnic table, with the nylon ropes through the grommets tied to the table legs. I went back to sleep. If he needed to get drenched in his own crummy tent, who was I to drag him back to someplace dry? That's why the thought of dropping my brother off at some schoolhouse and cooping him up like that makes me sick to my stomach. Plus, Tom would be mad at me for the rest of his life.

But you gotta do what you gotta do, Dad would say. Problem is, I don't really know what to do.

The branches are thrashing around in that wind and the string mop is banging crazy against the tree trunk. The moon is in my eyes like a flashlight, but I'm really tired. Just before I fall asleep, I think about Dad. Maybe he's in prison. I'll bet he's thinking about us.

I wake up to the sound of birds singing. I come up from way down in my bag and pull the hair out of my face and look around. Tom is over in the sun just outside the big shadow of the rock, writing in his notebook. I get

52

up and pee and drink some water and start to sing: *"Oh, she jumped in the lake to get away from a snake and said it would never find her. But the snake jumped in and the girl couldn't swim, so da-da da da da daaa da."* I wash up and look in the mirror to see how my beard is coming along. I had sunglasses on yesterday at the hot springs, and there's a band of white over my eyes. That gives me four different colors: the white band, my blue eyes, the black circles under them, and the sunburned rest of my face. I brush my hair. It's almost white-blond and goes nearly down to my shoulder blades. I put it in a ponytail for the hot day.

Tom comes over and shows me some pictures in his old notebook: stick people and an antelope, rows of lines and dots. "Remember this, Billy? It's the Indian writing."

Of course I remember. He drew them when we were here before, from me and Dad telling him what we found up at the top of the rock.

It was on the second day we were here. Tom was playing with a toy horse and some cowboys, and I was watching a wasp skittle along the ground covering up a hole with little stones. Dad was sitting in a chair until he got up and came over to where I was. "Hey, Bill."

"Hey."

53

"I got something we ought to do."

"What?"

"You're not gonna like it."

"What?"

He crouched down next to me. "You and me need to climb up this rock."

My dad knew I was afraid of heights, but I could tell that nothing I would say would make any difference. "Come on, Bill. You'll be all right." He told Tom we'd be back soon and to get in the Jeep if anything happened. He'd seen a good place to start up, and we put gloves on, and he brought a long rope, and we started to climb.

The way looked worn, like other people had done it before, but it was really steep. The sun was glaring, and the Jeep's rear bumper was shining out below like a mirror. When my bare arm touched the rock, and one time my cheek touched it because I was holding so close in, it burned my skin. My heart wouldn't settle down, and I was sick to my stomach. I was holding on so tight my hands and arms got tireder than they needed to. Dad looked down at me pretty often.

After a time, it got flatter and easier, and then I came up over a little rise and there was Dad sitting down in the shade, in a very small cave. "Hey," he said.

All around and above him on the dark gray rocks were white pictures, pecked out one little dot at a time by some people a zillion years ago. I whistled and took off my gloves and rubbed my arm where I'd scraped it. It would have been good to bring water, but we didn't. Dad lay down and hung his knee over a rock. I moved around and looked at the pictures. There were square box patterns and other squares made up of rows of big dots, each big dot the result of a lot of tiny, pecked dots. There were wavy lines and rows of wavy lines. There were stick figures of people with their arms out. There were lightning lines and footprint lines and snake lines and rainfall lines. There was one deer or antelope. All of it was clear but really worn into the rock.

I sat down. Looking out, all I could see was sky. Huge clouds had built up over the southwest, but the sun still blazed outside the cave. I watched the clouds moving closer and getting darker. There was some lightning on the horizon. It seemed very far away. Even though we were way up above the ground I felt like I was down underneath it, down inside a cave that was underneath everything. The place I was sitting in was a little seat made just for me. It seemed like I belonged there, and the whole world was up above, pressing me down with all its weight.

Finally, Dad sat up. He scooted over to the edge and sat there for a while. Then he turned around and smiled at me and wiggled his eyebrows. "Let's go, pardner." We started down, and when we turned a bend, I got queasy when I saw the Jeep. It looked like a toy car down below. I focused on where I was stepping and kept close behind Dad until he got to a tough spot, and I had to wait for him to figure out how to go. The clouds closed in above us and it got very dark. Thunder nearly broke my ears and lightning flashed close.

Dad was moving on, but I was stuck. I kept turning around, trying to go down backward like he had, and then I would turn around again and look down. I smelled rain and heard it splattering over the ground down below. Dad was waiting, looking up at me. I must have turned around five or six times and finally said the hell with it and dropped my foot onto something I hoped would hold me, and it did. I kept going, scraping my elbows and banging my forehead, and slid down next to him. He grabbed me around the shoulders and kissed my head and the rest of the way was easy. We ran into camp just as the rain hit hard. My brother was already in the Jeep, and we piled in too, and it poured.

"We'd have been down sooner, Tom-o. But Billy had

to do quite a dance on this one ledge."

"He must have done a rain dance," Tom said.

We slept in the Jeep that night because everything was wet. When I closed my eyes, it felt like the rock was next to my belly, and I could tell I was going to fall asleep easy. Right before I did, I heard my dad singing. *"Oh, she climbed up a rock to get away from a jock and said he'd never catch her. Da-da da da da, da-da da da da."*

The next morning Dad and me drew all the pictures we could remember in the mud to show Tom, and he copied them into his notebook.

Tom's got the notebook open to that page, so I'm looking at them right now. Tom is looking at me. "You want to climb the rock with me, Billy?"

"I don't think so. There's some hard places and you have to really reach and stretch. I don't think you're big enough."

"Yes, I am." He walks over and puts his notebook in the Jeep.

I move the chair more into the shade and sit down. When I look up Tom's headed for the rock. "Hey," I call out.

Of course he ignores me. He disappears out of my sight around to the other side.

Going over to look for him I walk past the Jeep and see the ground is all wet underneath the engine. I raise the hood and take off the radiator cap. There's some water in it but it's way down. We used up the Stop-Leak a few days ago. "Tom-o! Thomas! Help me with the Jeep." I wait to see if he'll come. He doesn't, so I close the hood. Then I crunch up through the rocks and around the corner.

Tom's climbed up about fifteen feet and looks to be stuck. Even that low, he looks small against the rock. He makes a few false starts and waves some bug away from his face and then starts stepping backward down. He slips, and I hear him yell. "Oh hell," I say and hustle up to where he is standing, bending over holding his head with one hand and his knee with the other.

I turn him toward me. He's crying and blood's running down his face. I don't have a shirt on, so I pull his off over his head and press on the right side of his skull. A dark spot comes through and spreads slowly. I take the shirt away and rumple through his hair and look. It's a gash and a couple scrapes, not too deep. "It's not bad, Tom-o. Let's go wash it." We walk back. Passing the Jeep, I see the wet spot under the engine is bigger and getting all muddy.

We clean him up and he takes a nap. I wake him to eat, peanut butter and potatoes. He goes to sleep again, and I go over and look at the Jeep. There's no water in the radiator. I go back to sit in the chair and watch the sky turn orange and red and gold as the sun goes down. The rock turns red and gold, and so do the trees, and after a while, it all gets gray. The temperature drops and I want to lie down in my bag, but I go over to the Jeep instead.

I get out our packs. We've got almost three gallon jugs of water left, and I put two of them into my pack. I wrap my jeans and three T-shirts and underwear around the jugs. My coat will sling over the top. I stand in front of the Jeep with no clothes on and pour a few sloshes of leftover water over my head and rub it over myself and stand there shivering while the air dries me. The moon's not up yet and the Milky Way is like somebody brushed a wide stroke of silver paint over the top of me.

I put on my shorts and my long-sleeve shirt and shoes and sit in the tailgate of the Cherokee and sort through our stuff. Pots and dishes we'll leave. Three Snickers bars and the peanut butter and a bag of dried milk I stick in my pockets to take. Knife, rope, flashlight, batteries all go with us. Cigarette lighter and matches. I find the envelope of important papers and put it in the bottom of Tom's pack, along with his notebooks and pens and his extra pants. I pull the blanket off the driver's seat and dig the package of weed out from the hole. It looks to be worth about six hundred. I wrap it in Tom's extra shirt and put it in his pack on top of the rest. It doesn't weigh much, and cops don't bother little kids, but it's on top where I can get to it quick and toss it if I need to. I stuff his jacket over the top of everything. His jacket is my old green one and I hold it up before I put it in. I can't remember when I was small enough it would fit me.

I sleep for a while and then wake my brother. We roll up our sleeping bags and tie them onto our packs and put quart bottles of water into the side pouches. Tom writes a note "Help yourself" to put on the box of pots and dishes that we leave at the campsite. He writes another note "Keep out" to leave on the Jeep's dash. We lock it up and split a Snickers and drink some water. Then we take off walking.

It's peaceful tonight, not windy at all. When the moon rises, we'll have bright light all night and maybe we'll reach the highway by dawn. There isn't a cloud any-where. I'll have to figure where to go without one, but there's only the one road out to the highway and turning west will get us headed toward Aunt Laurie's.

THE GIRLS

Miss Florida could have another orgasm, or she could get up and take the rollers out of her hair and start the day. Through the window, the day looked to be a fine one. A harsh sun was glowing beyond the sharp line of shade cast by the awning. Out in the yard, a lawn chair opened with a snap. Melba had the radio on, the volume considerably low. *Sin, sin, sin,* sang a woman's bluesy voice, *That's the trouble I'm in.* Miss Florida could not resist one more wave of sensation. She kneaded her ample lower abdomen and gyrated her hips. She breathed appreciatively into her long white legs, making sure the wave was given free run of the house, as she liked to say. It wasn't healthy to stop it.

"That girl you're so interested in's gone down into the woods again," Melba announced when Florida wandered out to the yard.

"How do you know? Can't see the woods from here."

"I saw. I was putting my sunshade in the car. She came flying down the hill with those cards in the spokes flapping away, jammed on the brakes, and tippy-toed in there."

Miss Florida laughed and pressed her finger gently on the end of Melba's nose. "Tippy-toed!"

"Well, she did, honey. That's what she did." Melba sat on a lounger, the heels of her tiny feet tucked between the aluminum edge and the webbing. She finished slathering Coppertone on her thin, bronzed belly between two halves of an orange bikini.

Florida pulled the front of her clinging gown away from her body and waved it in and out, fanning herself. "What shall we do today, Mel?"

Melba tapped her fingernail on the rim of an Old Fashioned glass that sat sweating on the ground beside her lounger. "I'm gonna start with this and see what happens." What had been ice cubes a few minutes earlier were now two frosty nubs fused in the inch of amber liquid left in the glass. "Super hot today." She lay back and covered each eye with a wet cotton ball. "Game's on at one."

"Oh, yes!" Florida walked around the edges of the small yard, deadheading petunias and snipping brown leaves off marigolds and pansies with a pair of manicure scissors. She drew a long, satisfied breath as the marigolds, disturbed, released a pungent odor. The scissors dropped out of her hand onto the ground. "*Redcap. Keeps the bears away,*" she said as she bent to pick them up.

Melba glanced at her. "That's what you say when you drop something."

"Right."

"Uncle Frank, right?"

"Yep."

Florida didn't mind the Missouri heat. It was like Miami, where she had been born and raised and where she had hoped to become Miss Florida in 1967. Her loss in the Dade County contest crushed her, but her pain was eased when she met Melba at the refreshment stand. Florida was getting a hot dog with everything; Melba, an iced tea. "You were great in the singing," Melba said. "It's all political anyway." Melba wore white Keds and madras Bermuda shorts that hung past her knees over the reddened sticks of her legs. Melba was not trying to become a beauty queen but came to Miami on vacation.

They liked each other, and within a few hours Florida was packing her things into Melba's Dodge Charger and riding up the coast highway to Jacksonville, where Melba had grown up and now worked in bottling at the new Anheuser-Busch plant. Melba was living with her parents. She installed Florida in a motel near the naval air station before going home to announce that she was getting her own apartment. Her mother wailed and pleaded and her father stormed. Their contorted faces made it easier for Melba to move out that very day. She visited them every week for a while, but after a few years she transferred to a job in billing at the headquarters in St. Louis, where she and Florida had been ever since, in a brick two-bedroom on Hemlock Drive in the suburbs. Phone calls with her mother dwindled to a few times each year. Melba liked her job, and her paycheck covered the mortgage, taxes, insurance, utilities, and maintenance. She paid the house off after thirty years and owned it outright. She had retired last year.

Deanna McElroy abandoned her given name after that weekend and adopted the one she thought she deserved, introducing herself as Florida, adding the "Miss" with people she would never see again. She kept the house very clean. She also shopped, riding the bus to the mall, bringing home clothes and trying them on in many arrangements before selecting a few and returning the rest to the stores. Sometimes she returned them all. When asked, she told people she worked in retail. She did volunteer at a local church thrift shop, sorting donations in exchange for a box lunch and fifty cents an hour to use in purchases at the store. She requested that they call her "Miss Florida," and they did. Her mother faithfully sent a small monthly check to Deanna McElroy, in whose name Florida had opened a checking account.

At first Melba was critical of Florida's shopping habit, but Florida defended it vigorously. "I pay my bills!" she hollered. Not entirely true in Melba's view, but not worth arguing about. She was happy when Florida was happy.

Miss Florida went inside. In the bathroom, she turned on the fan and pulled the rollers out of her hair. She brushed her teeth and put on lipstick, selected randomly from a jumble in the top drawer but applied with care. Even so, she got a dab of color just below her lip on the right side. She tried wiping it away and ended up with a gap. She repainted it and added a compensatory smudge on the left side. "Oh, baby," she moaned to the mirror, jutting out her chin and closing her eyes. She plucked her nightgown off over her head and brushed her hair, purple-red and full on the sides, then used a comb to tease the thinning strands on top. Despite the fan, rivulets of sweat trickled between her breasts. She turned the water on for a cool bath.

Melba went to the kitchen and replenished her Old Fashioned. She heard the water running and remembered Florida in the bathtub last night after once again wetting her pants, her face pouty under tears. Melba leaned against the kitchen counter and smiled at how quickly, how reliably, a much older memory occurred: their first night together, Melba and Florida took a bath together in a small motel off the highway in Vero Beach. Neither had ever done that before, and their initial goofy exuberance gave way to slow exploring as they soaped each other's feet, legs, backs and butts and bellies, genitals, arms and hands, breasts, throats. Then, washing their faces brought everything to a solemn stillness. Miss Florida washed Melba's face with languid care and honor and in turn allowed her own face to be handled that way. All questions were over.

Melba wetted new cotton balls under the kitchen tap and returned to the backyard. She stretched and looked around, then settled herself back on the lounger and put the cotton balls over her eyes. In the darkness, she saw the afterimage of the leafy bulk of the maple tree against the garage. Her mind was drawn fondly to the 1966 Dodge Charger inside the garage: black, sleek, ready to rumble. It was some years ago that she and Florida last took it out, heading west on Highway 50 on a cool spring afternoon. The car Melba drove every day was a 2008 Ford Focus, parked in the driveway.

She wiggled her toes and drifted toward light sleep. Another image came to her: a photo of herself at age seventeen, crossing her eyes at the camera. The picture was attached to an email she had received in January, an invitation to the upcoming forty-fifth reunion of the Jacksonville High School Class of 1965. The reunion was next month.

If she went to the reunion, she could also visit her parents, of course. In her call home last Christmas, her mother had told her that her father was not well. A troubled thought came: *I should've jumped on that hundred-fifty-dollar round trip in February. Tickets only go up in the summer.*

Florida returned to the backyard. "Well, I feel refreshed." She wore a sheer green T-shirt and very short white shorts that were more than filled by her hips and belly. Her hair bobbed in a ponytail as she scuffed across the patio in thong sandals with high cork heels.

Melba raised her head and squinted up at Florida. There was something in the way she looked at her that made them both laugh. She drank the dregs of her drink. The lounger creaked and tipped as she turned over onto her stomach.

Florida plopped into a chair. "Mel, what do you suppose that girl does in there? Why does she take a bicycle into the woods? I know she can't ride a bike in there."

"She doesn't want anyone to steal it. She can't leave it out there on the street. Maybe she puts it down once she gets in there. Just gets it out of sight."

"And then what? Why's she going into the woods?"

Melba shrugged. "Dunno. What's it to you? She's just a kid. She's playing."

"Playing what?" Florida stretched out her legs. She thought of the girl, cruising past their house on her bike with her arms crossed in brave satisfaction as she coasted hands-free past parked cars down the gentle Hemlock Drive hill. Skinny little thing, dark hair in a bob, white skin. About seven? Eight? Six? Red shorts or blue shorts, a T-shirt, white Crocs. "That little girl must be going to see somebody." She picked up the *West County News* and flipped pages. "Or else, she's going away from somebody."

Melba turned over a few times, slept and woke and slept. She wanted another Old Fashioned but didn't want to get up. Miss Florida stayed out of the sun. She played solitaire on an unsteady plastic table in the shade of the maple tree. There was no breeze to blow the cards away.

The phone rang, and Florida went to answer it in the bedroom. It was their best friends, Troy and Michelangelo, calling from the city to try to get Florida and Melba to leave the suburbs and join them in midtown—for a drink, for a movie, for an evening of canasta. Florida said she would like to but Melba would not; she was determined to become Melba toast and nothing could interrupt that. And the ballgame would be on. And she thought they had plans for the evening; she wasn't sure. Melba would know but now was not a good time to ask her.

"Who was that?" Melba asked.

"They wanted to sell us the paper. I told them we already get all the papers we want." Florida picked up the *News* and rattled it with a flourish, then settled into her webbed chair. "I'm thinking of going to the mall before

71

the game starts." The house, the thrift shop, and the mall were Florida's comfort zone. She picked up the *News,* opened to the crossword and slowly penciled in words. In a few minutes she spoke again. "Mel. A five letter word for *ruin*, last two letters are *C-K*."

Melba said something from underneath the Cardinals cap that covered her face.

"No, *fuck*'s only four letters. I thought of *fuck-up* but it's six and the *C-K*'s in the wrong place."

"*Wreck*," Melba enunciated loudly. "*W-R-E-C-K*."

"Yes!" Florida penciled it in.

Melba stood up and collected her towel, lotion, glass. "Well, it looks like you're not off to the mall."

"Should I not go? Do you have some interest in that?" Red six went on black seven.

"No, but you said you were going."

"Don't rush me."

Melba toweled off the sweat and slipped into flip-flops. "I'm going to have lunch." But instead of going into the house, she went and stood beside Florida. Her tanned fingers rested on Florida's white hand. "Honey, I wasn't pushing you or saying you should do anything. I was just simply saying it didn't look like you were going to the mall, after all. That's all."

"That's all after all," Florida said in singsong. "Miss Florida ain't a-goin to the mall."

Melba laughed, a harsh rasping burst. She plunked down onto the grass beside Miss Florida and the two sat in the late morning light. Melba stroked Florida's foot.

At one o'clock they moved the radio to the living room and switched stations to the ballgame. Melba made herself a pitcher of margaritas and sat on the couch. Florida turned on the fan and placed a blanket on the floor next to Melba. She covered her feet with the blanket and leaned back against the couch where Melba could fiddle with her hair.

They had to listen on the radio, not watch on the TV, because that was how Florida had done it as a child. She had listened to the Cardinals on KMOX in the 1950s, tuning in secretly at night under the covers to hear Harry Caray over the wires all the way from St. Louis to Miami as he announced the heroic deeds of Stan Musial, Curt Flood, and Alvin Dark. The only one Miss Florida had seen a photo of was Stan Musial, and she wasn't interested in that rugged face with the big nose. She pictured

Al Dark as black and husky and Curt Flood as slender and blond, and she loved them both.

It was necessary for Florida to tune in at the beginning of the game. She was sure that when she missed the start, it had a bad effect. Melba had tried to argue her out of this, but Florida had seen it happen too many times that if she tuned in late and the Cardinals were winning, they immediately started to lose. If they were losing, it immediately got worse. She had started watching games late in the sixth inning with the Cardinals ahead by eight runs, and by the top of the ninth, it was 12-8 in favor of the enemy team, as Miss Florida called them.

In the ninth inning the phone rang again, and Melba went to pick it up in the kitchen. "Hi, sweetie! Oh, did you call? Uh-huh. Okay, great! See you soon." She returned to the living room where Florida was curled up on the floor next to the radio as if it were a fireplace. "The boys are coming out. They've got stacks of sandwiches from Isabelle's opening last night." She headed for the kitchen.

Florida's mouth screwed into disapproval, and she followed Melba, carrying the radio. "You know, if I didn't even exist, they'd still come all the way out here. But if you didn't exist, I'd never see them."

"You'd be just as happy to never see them, as far as I

can tell." Melba started washing dishes.

"But they really are just coming to see you." Florida put the radio on the counter as a commercial came on. "Besides, Troy's a jackass. It's not that I don't like him—oh, he's likable. But he's a jackass. Last time, remember? He went on and on about that dog. *Oh, poor lady lost her dog,*" she whined. "*Oh, boo hoo.*"

Melba turned off the water. "What dog?"

"The dog! Some lady at the salon, the *Pahk Plahza.* Lost her dog. Big deal."

"I don't remember a thing about a dog, Florida. I remember Troy did a color on some woman whose brother committed suicide. The woman found him, dead in his car in the garage. Troy did go on and on about it. He did go on and on."

"Well, no, it wasn't anybody committing suicide. It was a woman lost her dog."

Florida took the radio to the bathroom. The game resumed. She stood in front of the mirror, putting her hair into a do, the radio on the edge of the sink. Albert Pujols was down in the count 0-2 in the bottom of the ninth, with two on and two out. Miss Florida glared at herself in the mirror, pretending not to care and muttering. "It's okay, you're okay, Albert. Walk the talk. Ready now— " She knocked twice on the wood framing the bathroom door.

"*There's a blast along the rightfield line!*" shouted the announcer.

"Whoo-hoo!" shouted Miss Florida. "Base hit! Go for two! RBI!" She smirked out the bathroom door toward the kitchen where Melba was washing dishes. "Whoo-hoo!"

"Sounds like you did it again," Melba called.

"Yes! We did it! Tie game! Oh god. They'll be here any minute and it's extra innings. Damn."

The game was over by the time the boys arrived. The Cardinals' defeat in the eleventh inning and the imminence of visitors started Miss Florida on scotch and water, and she was locked in the bathroom with her third one when Melba answered the doorbell.

"Lovely!" Troy gushed, wrapping Melba in his arms while holding his body away from her. "It's so good to see you!" Wearing tight orange jeans and a cropped white T-shirt, he stood grinning. His blond hair was spiked with purple and silver dye. He was barely taller than Melba but so muscular that he dwarfed her.

Michelangelo towered behind Troy, holding in each arm a round cardboard tray covered with foil. He was a foot taller than Troy and wore his customary knit slacks and button-down collar shirt. His large shoulders made his small head with its close haircut and trim, graying beard appear even smaller. He held his cheek down for Melba to kiss before carefully moving through to the kitchen with the trays. "Where's Princess?" he asked.

Melba nodded sideways toward the hall. "She'll be along. What are you drinking?"

"Princess! Princess Florida! Come out, come out, wherever you are." Troy skated his leather soles down the hall's hardwood floor and stopped outside the bathroom. "How are you, dear?" Waiting, getting no answer, he called to her again. "Florida?" Nothing. "Well, honey, we've brought food. I'll see you when you get here." He returned to the kitchen.

"She okay?" Michelangelo asked Melba.

"Oh, yeah. The Cards lost. And there's a little neighbor girl she's worried about."

"What's wrong with her? The little girl." asked Troy.

"Not a thing that I know of."

The three took food and drinks into the living room and talked about Isabelle's opening and Troy's plans to run a marathon. After half an hour Miss Florida left the bathroom, sidling first into the kitchen to make another scotch and then appearing in the living room.

"I was just primping, you know," she said. Her hair was not very artfully woven with an artificial braid and the mass hung over one shoulder onto her breast, which was partly exposed by the plunging neckline of a yellow quilted gown. Curious attempts at makeup had gone awry but remained, lending Miss Florida the effect of having an uneven sunburn.

"Well done, honey!" said Troy. He leapt to his feet and approached her, apparently unable to contain himself from making a corrective adjustment to her hairpiece. Michelangelo reached out an arm to stop him, and Troy held off.

"Florida, it's good to see you," said Michelangelo. He patted the couch next to him and she sat on the edge. "How are you?" he asked.

"I am just peachy keen," she said, reaching to place her drink on the coffee table. When Troy squeezed in beside her, Florida made a face, then stood up and looked brightly around the room. "How are you boys doing? How is city life?" She retrieved her drink and sat in a chair.

Michelangelo answered. "We're good, aren't we,

Troy?"

"Absolutely. Good, we are. I'm in training for the Chicago Marathon and Angelo's looking for a job."

"Oh, not looking very hard," said Michelangelo. "The bookstore is short this summer. I might do a stint there. Barry's traipsing off to some island for a few weeks."

"It's not a real island," said Troy. "It's got rocks for a beach and it's forty degrees all the time."

"It *is* an island," said Michelangelo. "You take a ferry to get there."

"Which leads to all sorts of jokes." Troy turned to Florida. "I'd like to traipse off to an island. How about you, Florida?"

"Well, of course I know Key West very well. Oh, it's a little bit of heaven there."

"Why don't you girls hop in that gorgeous old Dodge Charger and go find a ferry to take you to Key West?" Troy sucked on ice cubes from his drink. "Be good for you."

"I don't know that we want to go anywhere," said Melba, standing and heading for the kitchen.

"What about that high school reunion of yours, Mel?" Michelangelo called after her. "You were talking about going."

"She decided not to go," said Florida. "Too far."

Troy jumped to his feet and followed Melba. "Nothing

is too far for the Melba mobile." In the kitchen Melba said something he didn't hear. "Ummm?"

She waited until he reached her at the refrigerator and then whispered harshly. "Hush about all that. I can't take her, all right? Remember when she came to that party at Duff's?"

"Right," Troy whispered back. "Shhh." He pursed his lips together and raised his finger to them. "Spilled food all over and locked herself in the bathroom till the bartender threatened to call the police." He stepped back and helped Melba put ice cubes in a bucket. "You never go anyplace anymore. Will you ever get to retire? Holding her together is a full-time job."

"It's what I do." She moved past him.

"But why don't you go anyway? Fly. We'll take you to the airport. Florida can stay with us. We'll feed her and keep her on the terrace. You don't have to do it all alone." He held her face. "And you're drinking too much."

She made a face at him. "It's not a problem, Troy. I'm fine. But I'm not going anywhere."

"I can see that."

Troy and Michelangelo left at midnight. "Witching hour, dearies!" Troy exclaimed as the four kissed and hugged in the driveway. They drove away, top down, everyone waving until the boys turned the corner at the bottom of Hemlock Drive and were gone.

"That was fun," said Melba.

Florida carried dirty plates and glasses to the kitchen. "Well, except dear Troy Boy gave me a headache. He had to go on and on about me liking Albert Pujols's ass. *He's* the one likes his ass. I don't even see his ass. On the radio."

Melba washed. "Troy just likes to joke with you."

"He sits too close to me. He gets his face right up in my face. You know I don't like that."

Florida took the garbage out to the can at the curb. When Melba came out with glass and cans to recycle, Florida was squinting up the street. "Mel. I think that little girl's in the woods. I saw something move up there."

Melba looked up the hill and across the street where the short path, barely visible under the streetlight, disappeared into the woods. "What on earth makes you say that? She's a little girl, Florida. It's past midnight."

Miss Florida threw her a knowing look. "Little girls can go out very late at night sometimes, believe you me," she whispered.

Melba took Florida's arm and whispered too. "Okay. Let's go inside. We'll turn the lights out and watch from the window."

They did, and saw nothing but the faint, disordered blinking of fireflies. As they stood, Melba placed her hand on the small of Florida's back. It was warm and moist through the gown, familiar. Florida's hair tickled Melba's ear when Melba leaned into her and said, "She's not there."

Florida sighed and stepped back, never taking her eyes off the woods. She sat down and settled sideways onto the couch, leaning back onto the cushions.

"You're going to keep watching for her all night?"

"Well, somebody's got to watch out for her."

"Okay." Melba stretched and moved off toward the hall. " 'Night, Florrie."

"G'night, Mel." Florida's gaze was still on the woods.

Melba washed up and undressed for bed. Lying under the sheet, she thought of Francie, her high school friend who sent her the reunion invitation, and had a quick flash of Francie laughing at her across her childhood bedroom. Then, a vision popped up of her father turning away from her to go back to work under the hood of his Ford, the day she said goodbye before moving to St. Louis. Forty years ago, she cast her lot with Miss Florida, never thinking she and Florida would get old or that her parents would get even older. Melba placed her hand over her heart and whispered, "Miss Florida."

Alone in the living room, Florida gave up watching the woods. She tucked her hand under her thigh and thought about the evening. Troy was such a fool tonight. Brought those little sandwiches with the crusts cut off and slime inside, pink and green and orange. *"The pistachio's very good,"* she mimicked quietly. *"Nyah nyah nyah nyah nyah."* Mister Troy, he called himself. *"It's Mister Troy at the Pahk Plahza,"* he would say with a silly bounce of his hip. *"Mister Troy."* They had known each other for twenty years, and Florida never told them that she called herself Miss Florida. Troy would make fun of her; she could imagine his mocking: *"Miss Florida."*

She stroked her belly under her gown. "He's a creep, I tell you," she muttered. "He's a real creep." Then she added, "I'll never let him sit close to me again, I can tell you that."

Nothing moved up the street. Would the kid spend the night in there? It was possible. Florida was certain the girl was hiding. She thought of herself at that age, exploring the gully behind the school where pretty yellow flowers spread over the broken concrete and made a good field for her storybook dolls to play in. But not if that big boy was there. Little Deanna didn't like playing with him, but she didn't want to be at home where Uncle Frank might play with her.

"She thinks she can get away," she whispered to herself, stretching her legs and feet. Her toes just touched the cushion on the other end of the sofa. Her hand found its way to her crotch. She pushed it up inside the leg of her panties. Breathing deeply, she began to churn her hips and arch her back. Her gown scratched across her nipples. "She thinks she can get away," she whispered again. "But she cannot."

Miss Florida woke to the smell of coffee. She rolled over onto her back on the sofa. Melba had covered her with a sheet at some point, and she snuggled it up to her chin. "Hunh, hunh, umm," she hummed. "Umm, umm, hunh."

Water ran in the kitchen sink and stopped, and Melba came to the doorway. "I saw your little friend this morning," she said.

"The kid?"

"Uh-huh." She crossed the room to sit on the edge of the sofa next to Miss Florida. "She was riding that bike lickety-split down the hill here, making her little engine go with those cards flapping away."

"Oh, dear. Oh, dear." Miss Florida scrutinized the street.

"That kid, I think she's okay, Florida. I don't think you need to worry about her. I think she's just playing at her games, and she's okay. She's going to be okay."

Miss Florida smirked. "Okay, okay, she'll be okay," she said, singsongy. She turned and patted Melba's hand. "She'll be okay, she'll be okay. But what the heck shall *we* do today?"

They both laughed. "Coffee's ready," said Melba, standing. "I'm going out to spiff up the Dodge for a ride, Miss Florida."

"Oh goody! I'll get ready." She heaved to her feet and cast a glance toward Melba. "I get to go, right?"

Melba paused at the door to the garage. "Honey, I'm not going anywhere without you."

ROYAL FLUSH

O kay, so what if we're old? Is that such a crime?
No, there's no crime in getting old. I'm just
saying being old is a sad state of affairs. For one
thing, we can't sleep worth a damn. I'm just so tired of
being up all night. Aren't you?

Oh, it's okay.

She interrupted herself to concentrate on sitting up; she poked her foot at her slipper; on the fourth try, she got it on and hefted her heavy body off the couch. Bending forward at the waist, her belly pressing out the buttons of her pajamas, she crossed the room to the hotplate and heated up a tomato soup. She sat at the table to eat it out of the pan and continue the conversation.

No, there's no crime in getting old. The crime is in living through it.

She put the empty pan in the sink and returned to the couch. Picking up the remote, she put the movie on mute and tucked herself under a nubby beige bedspread, leaving her slippers on and her feet sticking out over the edge of the couch. She reached up and turned off the light.

So. Here we are again.

So what?

So nothing.

She closed her eyes and nestled the back of her head into the pillow.

Let's count sheep.

Okay. Where shall we start?

Start with number one. That college boy.

Drifting back, she found big suntanned hands, a glistening wristwatch. A plaid shirt, red and white and green, khakis coming unzipped, the softest lips. She was sixteen years old, working in her father's drugstore in Lawrence, a college town, in 1952. He came in to buy soap. He had the gift of gab and a thick shock of blond hair, and she had her father's truck. Sitting on a blanket in a field one spring night, her soft white leg stretched out from the little pleated skirt. No shoe on her foot. *Oh, oh, oh.* She sighed and diddled her fingers against the bedspread. A happiness.

He was number one.

She brought her new skills back to high school. Two, three, and four skipped past in a blur: a white pudgy tummy and wet hands; a yellow wool sweater that made her nose itch; freckles on a football player's hairless chest. *Oh, oh, oh.* And then number five, a snotty younger boy who made fun of her by acting like it was *him* who got *her* to do it. *Oh.*

The game was to remember as many as possible, to count as high as possible. But really the game was to pretend to want to stay awake, counting and remembering, and then to lose the fight and give up into the elusive fields of sleep.

She was getting there. Six, seven, and eight waved past beneath twitching eyelids: a campus radical with a beaky nose and bad breath; an older man who came through town every few months in his sixteen-wheeler, who kicked his feet. A funny skinny boy who told a knock-knock joke in the middle of it. *Who's there?* she gasped. *A little old lady*, he said, one thrust for each word. She knew the joke and attempted a yodel, and they fell apart laughing.

Her breath deepened and she went back to the count. Ten, he was that blind date. But she was bored with the game, and they got all out of order after that and started shuffling themselves like cards, jacks and kings of diamonds and hearts. Jack of the backseat of a new 1962 Oldsmobile. Jack of a screened-in sunporch in a closed-up summer cabin on a lake in October. Eleven, twelve? Thirteen.

She decided to focus on the kings of hearts, the ones who meant something. That would be number one—Bill or Will?—because he was her first, and it was so truly nice, the blanket, the night wind, the stars. She supposed there were stars but didn't really remember that.

Maybe she should count Ron as a king. They were together for two years. They were supposed to get married, and when he ran off to Colorado, she wasn't getting any younger.

But really it was a good thing because on the rebound she met number sixteen, the boy she did marry. The old woman's jaw slacked open, and her flesh softened along the back of her body. Dale, on leave from Fort Riley, and her sweet friendship with him over five days, before he left for Vietnam. Then two years of letters and waiting. She didn't really wait—she briefly added numbers seventeen through twenty-three or so, but they weren't kings of hearts. She wrote the letters to Dale and was glad to do so. Then he came back, and they married, and he *was* her king of hearts. She was his queen. He did very well in John Deere sales, and there were diamonds too.

After that, there were a few others, every one a jack. Until, to her great surprise, she met the queen of hearts. Who could have known there would be one whose shadowed eyes would talk to hers when she didn't even plan to be listening? Stroking, softly, small narrow limbs, such curly hair.

Oh, a happiness. *Clarissa, my love, gone to Heaven. Dale, my dear husband, my love, gone now as well. Bill, or Will. Oh, oh, oh.* Counting blessings.

She shivered and wiped her eye, then tucked her hand under the cover.

Are we asleep now?

Shhh. Almost.

THE FAMILY JEWELS

"If I've lost the damn thing, I've lost the damn thing!" Queenie was yelling at herself. "Stupid, stupid," she said from between clenched teeth. "You are the stupidest idiot." She started to throw things. Pillows and shoes at first, then books and the telephone and the jewelry box, and soon the whole dresser was about to go.

She stalked out of her bedroom and into the hall. She eyed the closet but couldn't imagine she would have put it there. She hurried through the screen door and down the few steps to pace the sidewalk that sliced through the backyard of stubby grass and weeds, slamming her bare feet down hard on the concrete. After half a dozen turns up and down the short pathway, she stopped walking, took a slow, deep breath, and sat on the steps.

The wind picked up and rustled the hollyhocks dying along the fence. Queenie clasped her shoulders, bare in a faded red tank top. Threads of the frayed hem of her blue jeans straggled across the tops of her feet. The thoughts kept running. *Shut up. You're so stupid. Shut up.* She dug a pack of Lucky Strikes out of her pocket, lit up, and focused hard on the paint on her toenails, Fiji Sunset.

She couldn't remember the last time she had worn the diamond ring that was missing. But tomorrow she would be seeing her cousin, who was her best childhood friend, for the first time in almost twenty years, and for weeks she had been planning to wear that ring. Now she could feel its absence on her finger, its pleasing weight a phantom on her right hand. A vague memory came: she had put on the ring and gone out shopping, then had taken it off before she went into the warehouse to pick up her paycheck. This was months ago—last spring? Last year? She had wrapped the ring in a Kleenex and put it in her purse. But she couldn't remember ever taking it out. At some time she must have cleaned out the purse and tossed all the wads of Kleenex into the trash. "It makes me sick to think of it," she said out loud. "I'm just sick."

She took a drag on her cigarette. The ring was her ticket around the world or her move to the West Coast.

Grinding her heels into the chipped brown paint of the step, she looked at her toenails again. She'd just applied the Fiji Sunset, a soft subtle mauve, still shiny and perfect. Inhaling again, Queenie silently counted as she released the smoke: *one two stupid idiot three stupid I hate four you I hate you stupid five stupid six idiot*. Blonde hair strung down across her damp face. She turned her foot inward, took a quick drag on the Lucky, and pressed the burning end against the wrinkled and scarred white skin of her sole. Holding it there, she exhaled. *Seven, eight, nine, ten. One, two, three, four, five.* She moved the cigarette away and held it between two fingers, gazing across the yard at the brown grass, the red fence, the gray garbage can.

The next day, in the lobby of the Seven Gables Inn, Maryanne saw Queenie before Queenie saw her. *What an oddball*, she thought. It was Wednesday morning, and the place was filled with men and women in subdued, sleek business dress. Queenie, her thin frame leaning to one side in a leather lobby chair, wore jeans and a green turtleneck that sparkled with sequins and metallic thread. White-blonde hair draped across her shoulders. She had a beaklike nose, and though she was seated, she appeared to be looking down at everyone. Dark eyeliner and mascara were incongruous with her pale skin and light blue eyes; lavender lipstick barely colored her small mouth. She sat with her legs uncrossed, knees together and pulled to the side. On her feet she wore sandals and bold-patterned socks.

"Sweetie, here you are!" Maryanne swept over to her. "Sorry to be late. Have you waited long?"

"Twenty years," Queenie said wryly.

Maryanne laughed. "Where can we go? I'm starving."

They walked a few blocks to a diner. "Nothing has changed." Maryanne laughed. "You were pokey when we walked to school, and I can hardly slow down enough for you now." She dropped her pace for her cousin and reached back to take Queenie's arm. They had walked to and from school together from kindergarten through junior high, when Maryanne's side of the family moved to Utah. Today was the first time since then that Maryanne had been back to St. Louis. Her husband, an ophthalmologist in the Air Force, had been stationed all over the world during his military career. They were settled down now in Arizona and were in town for the retirement of one of her husband's Air Force colleagues.

Maryanne's hair was the same dark brown as in seventh grade, shining and brushed back from her face. Her green eyes were narrow, her lips persistently pursed just as her mother's had been. Her stocky body seemed at home in a burgundy athletic suit. She wore Nikes and low socks that slightly revealed her tennis player's white feet.

Maryanne's mother had stopped speaking to her brother, Queenie's father, for some unmentionable reason that the two girls had never heard. Queenie spent a lot of time at Maryanne's house, but Maryanne's mother never allowed her to go inside Queenie's. They played castle under blankets hung between chairs in Maryanne's bedroom and later built forts with cardboard boxes in Maryanne's yard. On weekends during their last couple of years together, they rode their bikes into other neighborhoods or took the bus into the suburbs. Maryanne was funny, and Queenie wet her pants more than once laughing at her. But Maryanne could also be sweet, calling her cousin "Queenie Rose Garden," "Queenie Flower," "Queen Anne's Lace," or "Queenie Wildflower." She knew that Queenie never wanted to go home because her two older brothers were mean to her. So the girls would keep riding their bikes out late on Magnolia Street, past the quiet yards that smelled like watered flowers, and Maryanne would sing out, "Queenie Tulip! Queenie Beautiful Garden!"

Maryanne ordered a fruit salad and iced tea; Queenie, pancakes and coffee. When the drinks arrived, Queenie picked up her cup. "My god," Maryanne said and reached across the table to grab Queenie's hand. "What is *that*?"

"Oh, this old thing?" They both giggled as they looked at the large diamond on Queenie's right ring finger. "My sister came to visit a few years ago and gave it to me. Then yesterday I thought I'd lost it, but it turned up. Thank god. It was our Grandma Jane's. You remember my mom's mother married money, that banker? She left Lynnie six diamonds. Me being a black sheep of course got nothing. So Lynnie decided to give me this one. I had it appraised and it was worth a little more than what I earned last year. I had it made into this ring." The setting had cost Queenie five hundred dollars, which she paid for over time in six payments. The diamond dwarfed a circle of gold rose petals extending out around it. She moved her hand to the table's edge and watched the diamond glitter in the light of the lamp hanging over their table.

Maryanne thought, *she's made that exquisite diamond into a cartoon*. She looked at Queenie's hand and had a rush of fond remembrance. "Queenie Rose Garden, there's the Big Dipper!" She took Queenie's hand in hers and petted the constellation of freckles they delighted in as children.

Queenie grabbed Maryanne's hand and pulled it toward her. "Where's the eagle?"

Maryanne held her hand up sideways. She held her thumb tightly to her forefinger and crooked the finger into a beak around the end of the thumb. She lowered and raised the thumb to make the bird's mouth open and close. "Waw, waw!"

Queenie touched a vague dot on the hand. "His eye is disappearing."

"Faded with age," said Maryanne. She put her hand down. "Queenie, why did you say you were a black sheep? You were never that. You got the best grades of anybody. You never got into trouble."

"I don't know why, but I was. According to Grandma Jane, I was antisocial. Then when I grew up and had boyfriends, she said I was a slut."

Maryanne drank iced tea, rattling the cubes. "Well," she said. "As I recall, your Grandma Jane drank so much she wouldn't know anything."

Queenie had remembered where she'd put the ring only a few moments after burning herself. Stubbing out the Lucky on the top step, she ran back into the house and stopped before the door to her only storage space, a large walk-in that opened off the hall.

Carl had helped her move into the apartment, and he was the one who had stacked boxes onto the shelves and on the floor of the closet. In over a year of living there, she had ventured into it only a few times, with the lights turned on all over the apartment and music playing on the stereo: Mahalia Jackson singing gospel or Enya crooning Celtic ballads. Yesterday, considering the closet and where the ring might be in there, she rubbed her burned foot over the top of the other foot. Memories of another closet ran through her mind: the smell of her brothers' musty sneakers, and their armpits, mingling with their mother's Chanel N°5. Plastic bags from the dry cleaner waved in filmy silence above her, and one of her brother's hands pressed against her mouth. That closet had a small air vent high up on one wall, a square of parallel lines that she always focused on to take herself as far away as she could get.

She opened the door, pulled the light cord, scanned the shelves, and made up a song: "It's a different closet, not the same. A different closet, and I'm not to blame." In a moment she found what she was looking for, retrieved the ring, and stumbled back out into the hall. "Gotcha! Ha."

Queenie slurped coffee. "So anyway, I thought it was gone for good. But I finally remembered I had put it in the closet for safekeeping. I hid it in the popcorn popper."

Maryanne sighed in relief. "Wow." She leaned back in the booth. "You should go into that closet more often. God knows what treasures you'll find. The family jewels."

The waiter brought the food and fussed with making space on the table for an array of syrups in stainless steel pitchers. He poured Queenie more coffee. When the waiter left, Maryanne speared a piece of grapefruit. "So, what else is going on in your life?"

"Not much. But you've finally gotten to settle down. You lived in so many interesting places. Do you like Arizona?"

Maryanne made a face. "Phoenix isn't Venice, that's for sure." She ate a grape. "But I told you all about myself on the phone. Tell me about you."

Queenie gazed around the room. "There's not much to tell. I was with a guy for eight years, Carl, but he left last year. I work on call for a book company, in the warehouse, or driving little jobs around town. They give me quite a bit of work. It pays the bills, you know." Queenie's glance darted to the tabletop, the wall, the air above Maryanne's head.

Maryanne thought, *I could ask things. I could say, how did a straight-A student end up working in a warehouse? I could ask about Carl. What happened with him? Why did he leave? But twenty years ago, I never asked either. I never asked, what exactly are the mean things your brothers do to you that make you never want to go home?* "Queenie. Are you happy?"

"Happy," Queenie repeated, speaking to the tabletop. She picked up her fork and set it down again, then picked up the spoon and stirred her coffee. "Maybe not that much. But it's okay." She made the effort to look up at her old best friend. "Things have been a lot worse, and I really don't want to talk about that. So I don't know what to talk about." She buttered her pancakes and poured syrup on them. "That's nothing new, is it?"

The day after their visit, Queenie again sat smoking on her back steps. The weather was turning cold, and she wore a long sweater and jeans. Her toes, with Fiji Sunset, peeked out from under them. On her finger, the ring was heavy and startling. She thought it looked good.

She thought about Maryanne. "Let's stay in touch," her cousin had said as they were leaving, and Queenie thought, *we all know what that means*. But then Maryanne had taken her by the shoulders, looked at her, and said, "I really do mean that. I'm calling you next week."

It had been nice to have somebody to talk to, though she hadn't told Maryanne everything. She'd talked about how she'd stopped drinking, and a little about Carl. But she was too ashamed to tell about her violent attacks on him. Carl was a good person. There was no reason for her to scratch his face and cut his clothes into shreds.

These were not good thoughts. She took a breath without smoke and looked at her foot. She toyed with the cigarette before setting it down on the step. A tiny paint chip curled up and turned white under the lit end. She picked up the cigarette and took a last drag, tossed it onto the sidewalk, and went inside the house to make herself some breakfast.

THOSE KIND OF PEOPLE

Gary went to the register to pay for a packaged roast beef sandwich and a Rolling Rock and discovered his wallet was gone. "Damn!" Anger brightened his already ruddy face, and he groped his pockets but without hope. If he had it, he would know it. The wallet was a thin brown leather one, but attached to it was a jumbled cluster of keys half the size of his fist—to his house and shed and post office box, yes, but more than that. Six more keys, four of them marked *Do Not Duplicate*, unlocked his boss's gate and warehouse and machinery. These six keys and the boss he had had less than a month since being hired to do snow removal on the subdivision roads for the winter.

The woman at the counter saw the problem and bagged his items. "Hey, no worries, Gary. Pay me later."

Gary shoved the bag back to her and hitched up his jeans. They slipped down again immediately to their usual place low on his hips. "Naw, I gotta find the god-damn wallet."

He hit the door open with one arm and scrambled down the steps, jerking his jacket and T-shirt out of the way and reaching into his pocket for the Harley key. It was kept on its own embossed leather tag, separate from all the others. His foot slipped twice on the peg and he skidded in the gravel before getting the bike onto the road, leaving Brown's flashing neon in the dust. The wind cut into his ears and scalp, shaved except for a Mohawk stripe of white-blond hair from his forehead to a short ponytail at the nape of his neck. He quickly hit sixty, then seventy. His helmet, dangling on the handle-bar, swung back and forth as he leaned through the turns on the dark road that followed the river back into town. He knew exactly where the wallet and keys must be, if only they were still there. *Damn, damn, damn.*

Craig shivered in the passenger seat and turned around to see what was taking her so long. She was still inside the post office, standing next to the rows of boxes. Looking at the mail, he supposed. I'll count to ten and then honk the horn.

He did, and Kathy walked out slowly, studying something in her hands. She paused outside the Volvo in the parking lot light, bending stoop-shouldered over whatever it was, clumps of graying red hair falling down on both sides of her face.

"What the hell were you doing?" he said when she got in. "Close the door."

"Somebody left all these keys and his wallet. It was hanging from one of the boxes. The box wasn't even closed. It was empty, though." She squinted and read from the driver's license. *"Gary Snoodley, 674 West River Lane."* The face of the man in the tiny photograph was red and puffy. He had long blond hair, and he looked into the camera with two fierce eyes that didn't quite seem to match.

"What are you going to do with it? He'll come back. Just put it back in there."

"There's money in it." She flipped through a thin group of bills. "Two fives and two ones." She didn't mention a few other things she saw: a handgun permit, a Medicaid ID card, two sandwich punchcards for the local quick market.

Craig pulled his scarf tighter around his neck. "Would you start the car, please? It's freezing." He was rail thin and cold bothered him. His legs shook as he tried to warm himself.

Kathy started the engine and sat watching drops slide down the steamy windshield. "You know, River Lane is just down the hill from us." She backed the car out into the parking lot. "If somebody found my keys and wallet, I'd be glad if they brought them back to me."

"This guy must be a total loser to walk away like that," Craig tried. "Take it back inside, will you?" He sat looking straight ahead. "Other people were in the post office, and nobody else had to do a rescue trip."

She drove the four miles along the river and took the turn onto West River Lane, peering through the dark at mailboxes as she crept along the street. Houses were packed tightly together under giant cottonwoods. Some larger homes were raised on posts above flood level, but many shanties were tucked onto low lots that went underwater every few years. Kathy and Craig knew the street well. Many weekends in summer they walked through here on the way from their home on the hill to the county beach on the river.

She giggled. "It's probably the one under the bridge

with the dogs." Walking past that place on the way to and from the river was a trial, with three dogs lunging at a wire fence surrounding a dirt yard filled with disintegrating tools, car parts, and discarded household appliances.

Craig was not amused. "Will you just pull over for a minute?"

Kathy complied. "What?"

"I don't like this. You don't know this guy."

She didn't understand. "So what?"

"You've got his wallet. Do you think he'll believe you just found it?"

"Yes, why wouldn't he?" She rolled down her window and craned her neck into the night at a mailbox. "Can't read the number."

Craig snorted and opened the door. His loafer squished in the wet snow as he got out of the car.

"We're looking for six seventy-four," Kathy said. Craig slammed the door behind him and walked toward the next house.

Closing her eyes for a moment, Kathy gave a quick smile and then rooted hurriedly in her purse, took a bill from her wallet, and placed it with the bills in Gary's. "He looks like he can use it," she said aloud to herself. She cruised forward to pick up Craig.

It *was* the house under the bridge, with the dogs. "I can't believe it." Kathy laughed. She pulled into the drive, headlights shining through the fence onto a green Chevy truck with a heavy coat of rust visible in patches on the top and hood where the snow had melted.

The dogs started up, three black and brown mutts of different sizes, growling and barking and charging the fence. Lights were on in the small brown tar shingle house. A woman's voice shrieked unintelligibly as she came through the front door.

Craig took the wallet from Kathy and stepped quickly out. "Here come Fang, Bitch, and SonofaBitch. Wish me luck!"

Kathy watched him hurry to the gate as the woman, skinny in skintight jeans and a red sweater, came off the porch. "Hello?" she shouted and then began a coughing fit. Her hair stood up in white and blue spikes from her forehead, which was already unnaturally high. Kathy thought there was something good-natured about her. She looked like Bart Simpson.

"Is Gary Snoodley here?" Craig said loudly.

"Shut up, you damn dogs! Sparky! Elmore!" Bart Simpson came down the steps into the yard, her arms raised above her, a cigarette in one hand. "Who are you?

What do you want?"

She reached the gate, and Craig handed her the wallet. "We found this in the post office." He was already halfway back to the car.

"Thank you!" said the woman. "Wow! Oh, what's your name?" She stood staring.

"Craig," he called, climbing into the Volvo and slamming the door. The slush on his feet dripped onto the carpet.

Kathy rubbed his shoulder. "You made it," she said. "Thank you."

He exhaled sharply as if ridding himself of the dogs, the yard. "I'm sorry I told her my name."

"I don't think she'll come looking for you." Kathy backed out of the driveway and laughed as she started down the street. "But Fang, Bitch, and Sonofabitch might."

Craig laughed too.

Mary Jo hurried into the house and shut the door. She glanced down at Lucky, who was crawling across the linoleum. Dried tears and snot and sick baby exhaustion were muddled together on his face. None of it slowed him down.

"Don't chase the cat, honey."

"Daddy!" he cried. "Daddy! Cat!"

Gary would die, she thought, if he heard his name in the same sentence with the cat. She threw his wallet and keys on the table and lifted Lucky into the high chair. "Noodles, honey?" He banged his Spiderman cup on the tray.

What kind of people would search out their house in the night to return a wallet? Found the wallet at the post office. Why not leave it there? Meddlers, it would seem. Like the woman next door. More people to call the sheriff or the Humane Society. Well, they had no reason. "What kind of people, hmm, Luck?"

"Cat!" he shrieked. She shoveled food into his mouth and opened the wallet with her left hand. The first thing she saw was a fifty-dollar bill smashed around the other bills. She dropped Lucky's spoon and plucked out the bill, smoothing it on the table. Hope and anger rose in equal amounts: at the things that fifty dollars could do and at Gary for dealing weed again. She pursed her lips, ran her thumb over Ulysses Grant's forehead, and to her own great surprise started to cry.

&→

The post office was empty. The door to his box was wide open and the keys and wallet were gone. Gary bit down so hard that a piece of his lower front tooth gave way, pain searing into his lower gums. "Damn!" He yanked the broken piece from his mouth, stuffed it into his pocket and walked outside.

He stood under the streetlight, staring at his motorcycle: all right, time to sell you. He would get his uncle to fix the truck and go back to his hauling business. Or he would sell both the Harley and the truck to catch up on the rent and then go join his brother, who last week had gone to Baghdad on his second stint with KBR. Seven thousand a month, contract for a year. Mary Jo was against it, but things weren't working for him here.

Across the street he saw James, a teenager from his neighborhood, through the window of the pizza parlor. James was the one who started this mess, talking to Gary about bullshit when Gary was in the post office, making him forget his business. But James could sell Gary some weed, with money he would loan him, that Gary could sell for more money to the guys at the Palace in Laketown. Riding an hour and a half tonight and paying back James tomorrow, he could go home tonight with something: for Mary Jo, for Hunk. Mary Jo called their son Lucky, but

Gary called him Hunk. The baby's real name, given by his grandfather, was Mascot.

Craig tripped over the doormat on his way into the house. No one's fault but his own, really. The headache, though, was Kathy's fault. He had felt fine at the Piggly Wiggly and then until halfway through the video store, but she had to spend another ten minutes looking at Comedy even though they had already decided on *United 93*. After they left, he just wanted to drop by the post office and get home, but she had to get involved in somebody's drama. So now he had wet feet, a headache, and no mail. In her zeal to save somebody else, Kathy had forgotten to go to their own box.

He sat on the couch and took off his shoes. He looked at Gordon, the orange tabby curled up on a blanket on the coffee table. "These short days suck," he said to the cat. "Six-thirty and it feels like nine."

"What?" called Kathy from the kitchen.

"I'm talking to Gordon."

He stretched out and immediately drifted into sleep, not even noticing Kathy covering him with a blanket and then settling into a chair. Gordon padded over and jumped onto her lap. The room was silent except for the slight hum of the furnace until a branch fell on the porch roof. Craig opened his eyes. He wiggled his toes in their damp socks.

"There's a cup of tea. On the table, next to you," said Kathy.

He rolled over to face the back of the couch. "Thanks."

Mary Jo was lying on the bed in the dark when she heard the Harley. The bedside clock glowed orange: ten-forty-two. The baby was still playing on the floor, so she had turned the furnace on full blast.

Gary appeared at the bedroom door. "Meatball? You awake?"

"Watch out for Mascot. He's on the floor."

Gary sat on the edge of the bed, probing with his tongue the space where the tooth had broken. "Move over. Is there any dinner?"

"Macaroni's in a pan on the stove."

"Da-da-daddy," came a tired voice from the floor.

Gary dangled his arm over the edge of the bed and

boxed his son lightly. The child began to cry. "Oh, cut it out, crybaby."

"*You* cut it out," said Mary Jo. She stretched across his legs and pulled Mascot up by his arms. The baby wailed louder. She plunked him on the bed between them and tickled him, but he thrashed and screamed.

"Fuck," said Gary.

"Fuck yourself," said Mary Jo.

"Shut up!" he shouted. "Both of you!" His hand smashed roughly into Mascot's face as he pushed himself up from the bed.

Mary Jo shouted over the baby's screams. "Well, what do you want? He's tired. You came home a little late. He should be asleep."

"So why isn't he? Is that my fault?" Gary stalked around the room, then sat down again and pulled Mascot onto his lap, stroking the mass of red hair away from his hot, wet face. "Shh, shh, Hunk. It's okay." He shook his legs up and down, but the baby wouldn't stop his outcry. Gary gathered him onto his shoulder, stood up and glided around the room in a rocking dance. Mascot's wails dropped to a whimper and then stopped.

Mary Jo lay back on the pillow. "Some people brought your wallet and keys. It's on the kitchen table."

Gary stopped moving. "Jesus. What people?"

"Guy said he found it at the post office. Good Samaritans, I guess."

"Jesus." He sat down again and laid the child, asleep at last, in the middle of the bed. "It's all there?"

"All? I don't know. No money in it. Everything else is okay, I guess. I didn't really look. I doubt if anybody wanted your sandwich punchcard."

"Sons of bitches took the money and then brought the wallet back?"

"God, Gary, whoever took the money did it before these people found it. They were just goody-goodies." She stood up and yawned. "Come on, get some macaroni." She headed for the kitchen. "How much money did somebody get, anyway?"

"Fuck. Ten bucks or so." Gary followed her into the kitchen and sat at the table. He picked up the wallet and shook the dangling keys. "It's these I was worried about. It wasn't probably fifteen minutes before I got back to the post office. Stupid people should've left it there. How'd they know where I live? It was somebody who knows me?"

"Well, of course I'm only guessing, but could it possibly be from your name and address on the driver's license?"

Mary Jo set the heated pan on a potholder in front of Gary.

He speared yellow noodles. "It could still have been them took the money. Just to mess with me. Take the money and act like a goody-goody."

"They didn't act like they were messing with anybody. It was a couple. They were driving a very nice car, like a banker kind of car. Or a doctor. They weren't the kind to take twelve dollars."

He stopped eating and scrutinized her face. "Ten. I said ten."

"Oh, I thought you said twelve. Whatever. They were just goody-goodies, I'm telling you." She shrugged. "So where've you been? That was a long time ago they came by."

Eating had reminded him of his tooth. He pulled the broken piece from his pocket and put it on the table. "Son of a bitch broke off. I gotta get a job with dental." He pushed the empty pan across the table and picked up the keys again. "I thought I was totally out of a job when I lost these. So I made a little deal with James and some guys. Had to ride to Laketown. Had to bring home a little bacon." He wrestled a knot of bills out of his jeans pocket and dropped them on the table. "I wanta know who took my other money." He pushed his tooth around the wood veneer tabletop. "You said there was a guy?"

"Yeah. He brought the wallet up to the gate. There was a lady driving the getaway car. They were about a hundred years old. Why are you so into them? Some kids probably came into the post office, took your ten bucks, and then these two came along."

"I don't know," said Gary. "It wasn't fifteen minutes, twenty, before I got back there. I was all the way to Brown's, realized I lost it and went right back." He tongued the gap in his mouth. "Kids don't go into the post office."

"Somebody, then. Forget about it."

Gary thought back to how it had been: he had unlocked the box and left the wallet and keys dangling as he pulled out the mail and looked through it: grocery flyers, a bank statement, a card advertising an auction. He had thrown all of it in the trash can and then James was there, pimply wimp from down the block, and two even scrawnier teenagers, saying hi, how's it going. He told them it was going just fine, and they said yeah, we're gonna get a pizza and watch the Cavaliers beat the shit out of the Bulls, wanta come? He knew he couldn't afford a pizza and said no, he was going to get going, and he did.

It dawned on him, and he banged both fists on the table. The tooth hopped like a Mexican jumping bean. "Fucking kids! Fucking James took it! Goddamn it, that little rip-off shit." He was at the door. "That little shit rips me off and then sells me weed and makes me ride all night so I can make up what he stole from me. I'm gonna kill him."

Mary Jo got around him and down the steps before he did, skidding barefoot onto the clumps of dirty snow that corrugated the yard. "Stop it! Stop it! James didn't take your money!"

"How do you know?" he yelled. "Get away, for Chrissakes! Get back in the house." He picked her up by her shoulders and swung her around onto the bottom step.

She screamed, a long piercing shriek. "Wait, just wait, will you?" She stood crying and rubbing her arms where his fingers had dug in and then screamed again.

He stood staring at her. "You're nuts again. Get inside. Come on, let's go in. Come on, Meatball." He turned her around and hustled her up the steps, tapping his fingers on her hips. "Come on. I'll go in with you. Don't be nuts in the yard."

&→

Craig turned over again in bed, and the covers got more tangled. He kicked his legs and rolled over and punched the pillows into a different arrangement. He had gone to bed after refusing the chicken and vegetables Kathy had cooked, instead eating a bag of popcorn and a bowl of Rice Krispies, watching an episode of *Law & Order*. He knew he probably wouldn't sleep. He only went to bed to get away.

He didn't know which was stronger, anger or guilt. He shouldn't be so uptight. But she always made everything so complicated. He worked hard all week and wanted to take it easy on the weekends, and she ruined it. She didn't mean to; it was just the way she was. She didn't understand how hard it was to stay out of the poorhouse. He commuted three hours a day to a pharmaceutical company and spent all day there pipetting cells onto coverslips and squinting at research articles on the computer. The posture was bad for him. He tried three different chairs at the workstations, along with various cushions and footrests. He tossed down ibuprofen, and yet every afternoon at five he had to limp and slouch the four blocks to the bus stop. He slept on the bus until he was delivered to the parking lot for the ten-minute drive home. *This is not a life!* he thought. But his pension loomed like a carrot, only thirteen years away.

Maybe he wasn't a person who could live with some-body else. Divorced twice and nearly forty when he met Kathy, he hadn't planned to marry again. But her cheeriness was invigorating, seductive, and here he was: married again, for six years now. He thought he should apologize. He could get out of bed, go downstairs, and sit with her. He could hold her. But he did not. His breath was tight and heavy for a while, and then he fell asleep.

"No way." Gary stood at the kitchen table staring at the fifty-dollar bill, which Mary Jo had thrown at him with more shrieks and tears. "I didn't have that."

"Bullshit."

He sat down at the table and looked at her, seeing his son in her round pale scowl and dazed eyes. "You look like hell."

"Same to you." She sat.

"It was not in my wallet. That's the truth. Those people put it there, another trick or something. I don't get it. But wherever it came from, I can't believe you took it."

"I wanted to see if you were going to tell me about

it. And you didn't!" Her voice turned mocking. "'*Ten dollars.*' So much bullshit, Gary."

"I didn't have it." He closed his eyes and rested the back of his head on the chair.

Mary Jo paused, remembering how the fifty had been smashed into the wallet. Remembering, too, how Gary had told her the truth about selling dope in Laketown after losing his wallet, had shown her that money. She sat down with him. They had been together over ten years, since junior high school, and had already had all the fights: over money, over honesty. Suspicion flared up at times, but real mistrust had long since burned away. "Well, okay, where did it come from then?" she said. "Those people? What kind of people would put fifty dollars in a wallet they're returning?"

"You said it before. Just goody-goodies."

"I guess they're the kind of people who do things for people. The kind who let you go ahead of them in line at the grocery store. We must look like a charity case."

"Uh-huh." Gary was staring at the money. "Charity?"

"Yeah."

"I'm not a charity case." Gary tried to kick his boots off but could not and gave up. "I'm gonna call KBR tomorrow."

She stared at him. "No. No. Nobody wants you in Iraq. Your brother's got a skill. You can't do anything."

"They need drivers. Jerry took a second job over there, driving people around at night. I can drive. I can fix engines." He stood up and opened a kitchen drawer and rooted around in the clutter until he found a plastic baggie with two tubes in it. He brought it to the table. "Get that little mirror in the bathroom, will you?"

When she came back, he was using a toothpick to mix epoxy resin and hardener in a jar top. He put a dab on the broken piece of his tooth and had her hold the mirror while he put the piece back in place and held it with one finger. "Ahkhay," he said, and sat back in the chair still holding the repair, waiting for the bond to set.

"I can't believe anybody would put fifty dollars in your wallet," said Mary Jo. "Those kind of people would give CPR to roadkill."

Gary laughed, a funny sound with his finger in his mouth.

Kathy pushed a cart of books to a low circular reading table in the children's section of the library and sat down in one of the small chairs. The library opened in an hour. She was at work early to repair some worn out books and to be in this pleasant spot to think.

Craig was home, sick. He said nothing, but she could feel daggers of blame coming at her for his cold worsening. But there was no harm in taking the wallet to that house. Why did Craig have to be so mad about it? "Do whatever you want," he had said this morning. "Just don't drag me into it. Save the whole world but do it on your own time. Leave me out of it." She laughed out loud, a closed-mouth *hmmph*, at how mad he would be if he knew about the fifty dollars: throwing away hard-earned money, and on people like that.

Actually, she thought, *he was mad before I ever went into the post office. It seems like he's mad all the time now. When we first met, he would get mad about every little thing, but I'd joke with him, and he'd get right over it. Now he won't have any fun. Takes the bus to work at the lab at Wyeth, comes home on the bus, watches sports on the weekend, never anything we can watch together. He used to be sweet, somebody I thought I could be happy with. Maybe I'm just too different from him. He's afraid of being poor, afraid of being taken advantage of.*

She glued the damaged spine of an aging hardcover

and surveyed the single basement room that was the Woodville Public Library. It used to be a good county job. But she lost her benefits when they cut the library's hours back to eighteen a week, and they were talking about another cutback to twelve. Before marrying Craig, she had gotten along just fine, but now this job would never support her and it would be twenty years before she could collect Social Security. Well, there are ways. She had always been able to find work. Not for the first time in their marriage, she thought about where she would look for an apartment, maybe a trailer park.

Two years later, on an Indian summer day, Craig was lingering on the porch outside Brown's Market before walking home. He had spent an hour reading a book at the river and was deciding whether to buy a Sunday paper. He thought too much reading might give him a headache. Cars came and went in the parking lot; people trotted up and down the steps dodging three shirtless teenage boys who were kicking around a hacky-sack. The screen door slammed often.

Someone called out. "Snoodley! How's it going, man?"

Craig looked up from the newspaper machine and saw two men backslapping in the parking lot. He hadn't thought about the wallet loser since the house under the bridge had been abandoned shortly after the incident that Christmastime. He bought a paper and moved to the end of the porch, closer to the conversation in the parking lot. He leaned on a post and studied the front page.

"I heard you were in Iraq, man," said the one who wasn't Snoodley.

Snoodley was tall, muscled, well-tanned. His blond hair and beard were trimmed short. He stood relaxed in khaki slacks and a navy blue T-shirt, talking to the other man. Craig couldn't hear his words.

A woman got out of a blue SUV holding a little boy's hand and went to join the conversation. Craig recognized her, though she had changed. Her hair was a decent cut and color now—shoulder length, cattail brown. She'd filled out and looked very good in tan capris and a white T-shirt.

Snoodley put his arm around her. The boy grabbed his legs, and Snoodley rubbed his hair. The other man bent over to tweak the kid on the chin. "Gary, Jr.! Nice to meet you."

Traffic disappeared for a moment and Craig heard Snoodley's words: driving for Buckeye Transit, two trips a day to Toledo. Pay's okay, good benefits. Mary Jo's got a daycare business. Little Gary starts preschool Monday. Then a pickup with a bad muffler pulled into the lot, and Craig couldn't hear the rest of the conversation. The two men shook hands, and the other man left.

Snoodley and the woman and child got into the SUV. They talked. Snoodley looked in Craig's direction and got out and approached the porch. Craig started to leave, but Snoodley came right up to him, blocking his way. Craig was as tall as him but half his muscled bulk.

"Excuse me," Gary said. "Is your name Craig? My wife says you're the person who returned my wallet a couple years ago."

"Oh, no, it wasn't me."

"You sure? She's sure it was you. House under the bridge?" Gary gestured that direction. "You found it in the post office."

"Oh, yes, that. Yes, my wife found it."

Gary pulled his wallet from his pocket and pulled out a bill and offered it. "I want to thank you. Here's what you gave us."

It was a fifty. Craig's face clouded and he took a step backward. "You don't owe me anything."

"Look, you helped us out and now I can repay you. Take it."

128

"There's no reason for this. I don't want your money." He had stiffened and was moving around Gary. "Excuse me."

"Well, I didn't want yours either, but you didn't give me a choice."

Craig just wanted to get away from this man, but for the first time he looked him in the face. He saw nothing threatening; the man seemed sincere. "I'm afraid I don't know what you're talking about."

"You didn't put fifty bucks in that wallet before you brought it back?"

Craig shook his head no but simultaneously thought: *Kathy*. "It might have been my wife. My ex-wife. I don't know. She didn't say anything about it." He pursed his lips. "But she might have done that."

Gary smiled and again offered the fifty-dollar bill. "Well, give it to her, then."

Craig hesitated. Gary folded the bill and gently placed it in Craig's shirt pocket, turned and walked down the steps back to his car. Mary Jo smiled and waved at Craig through the window as they pulled away. The little boy was in a car seat in back waving his arms, flying a toy airplane around in the air.

CRYSTAL MONKEY

The whole armful of logs slipped out of my grasp and dropped all over the three steps going up to my house, grazing my arms and shins and bouncing hard on my foot. I danced backward and just caught myself from falling. "Goddammit!" I sat down on the top step and rubbed my toes, bare in Birkenstocks.

A few pieces of wood had dropped down beside the steps and landed on top of the flowers next to them. The mashed nasturtiums gave off their sweet scent and made me crave a salad, but the thought of food immediately made me nauseated. I couldn't tell the nausea from the boil of anger driving my stomach up into my chest. "Goddammit."

Mitchell came around the corner. "Charlie! You lost your heat for the night."

"Almost lost my lunch, too, and cut the hell out of myself." I fingered a scrape on my forearm.

He laughed. "Don't bleed out on me, bro." He nudged me to scoot over and sat down next to me.

Mitchell is my best buddy from Vietnam. He grew up here in Gunnison, couple hundred miles from Santa Fe, where I grew up. We were two mountain and high desert boys in a squad together in the jungle, and he saw all the worst of what I saw. We've always stayed in touch since then. Eight years ago I was living in Alaska and came here to see him on a visit and decided to stay. I got a job doing maintenance and gardening for a small school out in the mountains. I built a cabin for myself on Mitchell's property. Since last year, when the cancer came and I stopped being able to do my regular job, I still do what I can to help him around here. Mostly, now he helps me.

I looked down at the end of one of the logs I dropped and saw the track of the chain saw. The wood was good and dry from three years before. Mitchell and I spent that summer in the national forest cutting logging debris. We would jeep out there into the West Elk Mountains and stay for a week or two, cutting all morning and spending all afternoon up at some lakes and snowfields and meadows of Indian paintbrush. We sold a lot of the wood, and we were still using it ourselves.

He picked up the logs for me and stacked them inside next to the stove and then took off. I didn't want the damned fire anymore. But night was coming and I'd need it soon, so I pulled up a stool, opened the glass door, and set it up. Then I went and sat in the chair by the window, to die some more.

Everything makes me mad these days, ever since I'm back in my regular life after my trip. I fitted out a van last spring, and for most of July and August I went down to New Mexico. I drove down along the west edge of the Sangre de Christo Range all the way to a meditation center, where I lived in the late 1960s. I wanted to visit the place one last time.

I stayed for three weeks, the first time back in all those years. I knew that a lot would have changed since 1969. A wildfire burned most of the place down twenty years ago and a lot of the buildings were new to me, but two of the original ones were left. The central dome made it through the fire, and the old kitchen. I was happy to see them. There were some new creaks in the kitchen floor, but I found the old ones too: you still have to take a large step just inside the door if you want to avoid a really loud one. The porches and the stone walkways felt the exact same way they used to under my feet, and also the slope of the driveway. Three clotheslines were still drooping on the same iron poles.

But something there has been lost. Fifty years ago, a small Hanuman statue made of pure crystal, not more than six inches high, was sitting in a shallow round dish filled with dirt and planted with some tiny cactuses, of all things. He sat with his prickly companions on a little platform near a window in the kitchen. Hanuman is a monkey, the Hindu god of devotion and kind of a mascot for that meditation center. He stood by Rama, god, to overcome the forces of evil.

My friend Susie gave that statue to the staff as a gift. I thought he would always be there. But fifty years later, he's gone. When I asked about him, no one on the staff now had ever seen him. He belonged to them — or so Susie intended — but they didn't even know about him. They looked around, but he wasn't there. "The fire," they said.

It wasn't the end of the world for me, but I wish I had been able to see him again. The kitchen survived the fire, so he should have too.

I first heard about the meditation center right after it started. I was twenty-three years old in 1968 when I ran into my old high school basketball buddy in Santa Fe Plaza and he told me about the place. Susie, his little sister, was one of the people starting it. I had always liked Susie, not romantically but just ordinary liking. She was too smart and tall to be popular in high school, but she kept her head high and walked through the halls as if she belonged anyway. So I decided to drive on over to the Sangre de Christo to see what she was up to.

When I got there it was late summer and they were getting ready for their first winter, and the water heater in the kitchen was giving them problems. I started working on it with a guy named Paul who wouldn't talk to me much because he thought people who meditated should be quiet. I found a rusted valve, and we rooted around in the cluttered maintenance shop until we found something that would work by adding a couple of washers, and we got the thing fixed. That evening Susie and I drove to a restaurant, a long trip on dirt roads. We got into playing a video game called *Pong*. She went at it like a holy terror and said "Shit!" a few times when she missed. I knew then that the meditation hadn't ruined her.

I stayed for a year. They needed somebody who could fix things, and I liked living there. I found out that I really enjoy sitting and meditating. No matter what's happening inside your head or outside in your life, you can just sit down and take it easy, not worry or try to figure it out or do anything about it. Two years after leaving Vietnam, I was still getting used to being away from it. The meditation helped with that.

I was in the office with a few other staffers the day Susie gave the monkey god to the center. She came in holding a cloth bag. "I want to give this to the staff here. It's for everybody who keeps this place running." She opened the bag and pulled out this exquisite small Hanuman statue. She placed it down among the piles of papers on the desk in front of the manager.

Everybody in the room went over to look. There wasn't a flaw in the clear shining glass. It was perfectly sculpted with the elaborate folds of the robe draping over the even, relaxed sitting posture, the neck and arms hung with beads and bracelets, the elaborate crown sitting over curls of hair. His head was topped with a miniature temple and backed with a fluted halo. His eyes were looking slightly downward. The fine shape of the hands rested palms up, on his knees. The tiny fingers seemed like they belonged to a real living person. He was somebody you would want to know: a gentle smile of utter benevolence softened the bearded monkey face. The shining of the crystal was so bright, and yet his face and the way he sat were so very quiet. I could almost feel his breath moving in my own belly. His monkey tail curled from the back onto his lap.

"Wow. That's beautiful," somebody said, and everybody agreed. "Where'd you get this?"

"Aunt Viola. A few years ago I was at her house and saw this gorgeous little god sitting on a shelf. I had never noticed it before! My great grandmother was a missionary in Asia, and Viola had a lot of artifacts she got from her. I saw this crystal statue on the shelf, and I was oohing and ahhing over it, and my aunt gave it to me."

"You're giving it to the staff? You're giving it to yourself, then," the manager observed.

"Yep. And to you," she said to him. She looked around at each person. "And you, and you, and you, and you. And also to me." She folded up her empty cloth bag and headed for the door. "And it's for all the other people who come to work here in the future."

I thought a glass monkey was a perfect gift for the

staff, who were so much less visible than teachers. Teachers sat up in front and told you things. You couldn't miss them. But the cooks and managers and maintenance men did everything behind the scenes. You could almost look right through us and not even see us.

The assistant manager made the Hanuman a nice seat in the wide dish among the cactuses. I built a manzanita wood shelf and secured the dish to it and mounted it on the windowsill in the kitchen.

I liked Susie. I'd walk through the kitchen and see her stirring a huge wok of granola or shaping dough into thirty bread pans. We were both busy, but we found time to talk, usually in the kitchen but sometimes in her room or mine, or taking a walk. She told me she had learned to cook from her Aunt Viola, who was mean to her, yelling at her for breaking a cup and chasing her up and down rows of sheets hanging to dry in the basement in winter. I told her I learned about fixing things from my father, who yelled at everybody and hit me and my mother. I also told her more about Vietnam than I ever told anybody before or since and how it's been for me after I left: life is so precious, yet nothing matters very much.

Mice were coming into Susie's room at night, and she asked me to close up some holes in the wall. I drew pictures of friendly mice on the boards I used, and she made me a fat cinnamon and sugar mouse out of leftover pie dough. Its tail broke off in the baking, but I was charmed.

At Christmas she invited me to come to her parents' house over in Santa Fe. My own family didn't exist, and Susie had a big family. A lot of their friends came over too. Of course I already knew her brother, and her mom and dad made me feel very welcome.

On Christmas afternoon her father went into a closet in the hall to get something, and he came out wearing a Cossack fur hat. We all got into trying on the hats in there. Why so many hats? Susie put the Cossack hat on me, and I strutted around. Her mother looked great in some kind of uniform cap with braids on it. I liked Susie best in a faded blue beret with a tassel. Aunt Viola was there, but she wouldn't try on a hat. She asked Susie how the little crystal statue was doing. Innocently, even cheerfully, Susie told of giving him to the staff.

On the Greyhound bus back to the meditation center Susie unwrapped the lunch her mother had packed for us. She handed me a cheese sandwich and said, "Charlie, I'm really attracted to you."

I looked at her and nodded and then looked past her out the window. I wondered: how could that be?

We started eating and she giggled. "That's it?"

"What's it?"

"Nothing, I guess."

During my visit to the center last month, I found my way off the beaten path to a formation of rock ledges and grass that we used to call the Rock Arroyo. I walked barefoot on the grass and lay on the rock. I had brought a baggie of sunflower seeds with me like I used to, and I fed droves of chickadees. I laughed, and also cried, at the little feet curling around my fingers, the sharp striking of beaks in my palm, the flutter of their coming and going. The little black eyes, seemingly quite awake, looked at me with great interest.

The Rock Arroyo was the place where Hanuman lost his head. Carpets of flowers came out in the spring. Susie took the statue out there one day to take some photographs of him in the rock niches, and she invited me to come with her. She wrapped him up in a cloth to carry him, and when we were leaving she reached to take my hand. Hanuman slipped out of the cloth and fell onto the rock. He was totally undamaged except that his head broke right off. I picked up the two pieces. Susie was shaking her head and saying, "No, no, no." She grabbed me in a hug and started to cry.

I put my arms around her, holding the statue's head in one hand and the rest of him in the other. The head hardly weighed anything and had a nice cool feel to it. "It's okay, Suze. It's a clean break, no lost chips. We can fix it."

She cried more, couldn't stop. After a while she settled down and pulled away from me. "Not okay. It's not. I'm so careless. I break everything."

I crouched over to look into her face. "You don't break anything. Hey —" I waited for her to look at me. "You don't break anything. You never have and never will."

She kissed me, a sweet small touch on my lips. "Charlie."

Later that day I offered to glue his head back on, but she wanted to do it herself. I gave her some Superglue, and she fixed it really well. You couldn't even see the crack.

Not long after that, Susie went back to Santa Fe for her aunt Viola's funeral. When she came back, she told me that the crystal Hanuman cost her thirty thousand dollars. Actually the statue didn't cost her that. It was giving it away that cost her that much. "Before she died, Aunt Viola took me out of the will. My mom told me that Viola was going to leave me thirty thousand dollars but she was afraid to leave me anything because I might give it away to a cult." Which Susie would not have done. "I might have given *some* away, but I would have been quite appreciative to have most of that money for myself."

Now that the Hanuman's disappeared, the whole thing might be seen as a case of karma. Aunt Viola was disappointed that Susie didn't keep the gift she gave her. If Susie were here, I imagine that like me she would be a little disappointed that the staff at the meditation center didn't keep her gift to them. So the crystal Hanuman is riding around on the great wheel, showing us that what we do is done to us.

New staff came during the summer, and in the fall we all went our separate ways. I went to Flagstaff and then to Austin, Texas, and then to Alaska, living in a lot of different places up there. Eight years ago I settled here in Gunnison. This is how I've lived my life — not much holding me anywhere, a little job helping people out in a decent way, a fair amount of time. When I was born, it was like some airplane pulling a glider up into the sky, and my life ever since has been drifting through the days and nights with hardly any sound, on long slender wings, flying around in big useless circles.

Through all that moving around, I've stayed in touch with some of my friends from those days at the meditation center. The assistant manager is in Australia, and another of the maintenance men is in Switzerland. Quiet Paul moved to Boulder and ended up being my friend for many years until he died last spring. He heard that Susie moved to Hawaii and started calling herself Susan. She got married.

I wonder where the statue is sitting now. He may be shattered. Or he may be upside down in a landfill resting on a rotting dead raccoon, shoulder chipped, the head long since broken off again. His head might be a serene crystal monkey face smeared with rancid mayonnaise, lying intact beneath the United States of America trash heap.

I miss him. I don't care where he is or in what condition. I would like to touch him and let that chunk of glass affect me in whatever way it does in the moment, right now. I'd like to see him whether he's sitting honorably on someone's windowsill or busted up in a trash heap.

I'm thinking about advertising to find him. I could put a classified ad in the spiritual journals. Finding it could be my last work in life.

Some spiritual people might say I'm attached. I don't feel I have to explain myself, but I'll just say this much: matter matters. The crystal Hanuman has a story and is connected to all sorts of people in ways known and unknown. Something is telling me to search for it. All my life I've followed whatever I knew, inside, I had to do. I'm actually not attached to the thing itself. If I had it, I could as easily throw it hard against a brick wall or drop it into the Pacific Ocean, if that's what I felt was called for. It's the wind, not the guy inside, that tells the glider where to go.

Living has been good, but I haven't fought very hard against this cancer. I did a little of this and that, some reading and talking to people, and I decided not to do all the treatments. At first I was freaked out about dying, but I've gotten used to it. It isn't that big a deal. But as dying gets closer, sometimes I cry. Who wouldn't? Small things take on big proportions, and I get sad about going. For example, I hope I get to see the start of the NBA season.

I've seen a few people die, and most of them weren't

ready. The first person I saw, when I was in high school, was a stranger. I was in the next car to come along behind her accident. She was waiting at a traffic light when a pickup truck went through the red light from the opposite side and mowed her little car down. I found her smashed between her steering wheel and seat. She must have been putting on lipstick when the truck hit because the empty tube was lying on what was left of the dash, and she had a dark ruddy streak smeared from her lip up across her cheek and the corner of her eye and ending up in her hair. She was breathing at first, but I was working at opening up the door and the next time I looked at her, she wasn't.

The next people I saw die, quite a few, were in Vietnam. One was our radioman. Mitchell was with me when Francis stepped on a mine. He was blown apart but still screaming. We both knelt over him, and he grabbed our hands and smiled at us. Then he was gone.

Who was ready? Not lipstick lady, probably. In Vietnam all of us knew we might die, but I know I wasn't ready, and I doubt anybody was.

Last year I was with a dozen other people sitting with Paul, who decided he had lived long enough with a brain tumor and would eat some yogurt laced with death, in the company of a compassionate doctor and some friends. Paul said he was ready. He had gotten happier over the years, but I watched the brain tumor replace his happiness with fear. His gray brow rumpled into long-standing grooves as he told me that some sadhus and swamis said the rebirth after suicide would be terrible, and there was a funny little look of doubt that crossed his face not long before he swallowed the yogurt. He looked really happy at the very end, though.

A few weeks ago, I started making clay pots on Mitchell's wheel. The pain is getting worse every day now, and the wheel was too much after a while, so I just fooled around with lumps of clay and ended up with shapes I liked. Charlie's turds, Mitchell calls them. They're sitting along the bottom of the fence like some big mammal traipsed through and left droppings every few yards. Every time it rains, the turds disappear a little because I didn't bother to fire them. Mitchell says he's going to fire one to save as a symbol of me after I'm gone. That made me think of my body getting fired. Most people I know of get cremated. I guess I will. It's probably against the law, but somebody should take the ashes up in a glider and drop them out.

I wish, really wish, that I could just sit out in the

rain and wash away. But lately I've been thinking I need to find another way. I'm gaunt and shaky and starting to turn yellow. It's time to get ready, if there is such a thing. I've been listening to know where the wind is blowing, and more and more I understand. It's getting very simple.

I'm wondering if I want a friend to be with me. Paul had friends with him, and I believe it was good for Francis that Mitchell and I were there. Then I started wondering if I have any friends. Friend being somebody I could tell the truth to and vice versa. Tell and also show. I listed my friends to myself and found that I do have some. Most of them are spread all over the world. Mitchell, of course, is right here, and there are some other people around here. Cancer is a big sign that says somebody needs help. Neighbors and people I used to work with have come to see me, brought me food, given me rides. Given me company and comfort. But even with all the help, I still find myself alone a lot. That is my choice and usually has been. I do truly like it.

Yesterday I told Mitchell I might want his help. "You got it, Charlie," he said.

"I need you to help afterward. Call 911. It won't be bad. A twenty-two only leaves a little exit hole. I'll go outside, just up the hill. Up by the big rock. It'll be sometime soon, probably in the next few days. I'll let you know." I know exactly what tree I will lie under, exactly what old red blanket I will wrap around me.

His mouth went into a tight straight line, and he nodded yes. "No problem." He actually teared up. "I can handle after. And I'll be there with you before, and during, if you want."

Looking at him, I saw right through the mostly bald, very wrinkled, blotchy-skinned old man, and there he was from before: square-jawed, crew cut, blue-eyed, smooth-faced, handsome twenty-year-old. I smiled and told him I loved him.

I don't think I'm afraid to die, but this morning I cried hard. I lay on the floor wailing and rolling from side to side, first whimpering but ending up sobbing and wailing like a baby. I don't think I could cry like that with anybody around. Some things I have to do alone.

All of a sudden I thought of Susie. I wondered if I could cry with Susie, and it hit me hard: she really loved me. A big wave of tears came, but it passed right through me in an instant. Very quickly the anguish was gone, and my body got quiet. Susie seeped into me. Her touch, that one little kiss. The way she said my name: "Charlie." The hard floor that was under me felt like a warm hand holding me, and everything settled down inside. I fell asleep.

Sitting here now at dusk, I'm not in pain. I'm fed. Not scared, not mad. I like sitting here doing nothing at all, watching the sky and trees turn gray. My cabin has a lot of windows. I'm going to let it get really dark before I light the stove. If the crystal Hanuman were around, he could be sitting here in the window with me, quietly letting the daylight dance through his skin. I did write a classified ad but haven't sent it in yet. I can tell I won't be completing the task of finding him. The timing isn't right. And I don't have anyone who especially would want to carry it on after me. The crystal Hanuman and I are very insignificant.

Still, if somebody, anybody, wants to take on this foolish but heartfelt quest, please do. He is about six inches high, Hanuman sitting in the meditation pose. He is the most beautiful pure crystal. The head broke off, but you could hardly even tell because it was glued carefully on again by Susie.

IF YOU LIVED HERE

"There's a house for rent in Duncans Mills," I say, mousing the cursor to the right and clicking. "It looks good! And it's in our price range."

My husband is making cheese sandwiches and doesn't come over to look. "What time are they coming?"

"Two." I click through photos of rooms with arched windows looking out on trees. I notice that another house sits very close next door, and then I see the home is right across the river from the gun club, where they start shooting at three o'clock every afternoon and at ten in the morning on weekends. In the list of the house's features, I read this: *Flooded only once in the past two years.* I shut the laptop and stash it between two coats lying on top of a large box in the closet. Some potential buyers are coming over to look at our house, so I get ready to leave for a little while.

Our house is for sale, and there is no place we want to move to. It's a dilemma, but we go ahead trying to figure it out and making confused efforts at packing. Late bloomers, busy with life's adventures and blissfully established in financial insecurity, we never thought to buy a house until we were already a little old. But fifteen years ago, we managed to afford this little gem, paid it off, and have loved being in this place of solitude and natural beauty.

Now, though, as will happen, we are progressing in age and regressing in functioning. Our only income is paltry Social Security, and our savings are dwindling. We can't keep up the maintenance or afford major repairs, and navigating the road and the steep stairs is getting harder. Our house is located at the end of a dubious driveway on a steep slope and has a leaking roof and an aging, problematic septic tank that, strangely, is situated higher than the house. We constantly need to clear brush from the roof and repair crumbling cliffs above and below. The final nail in the coffin—not a good metaphor—is the drought-driven increase in wildfire danger surrounding us.

So we've decided, sort of and reluctantly, to sell. "It's a good time for us to leave," I say to my husband. "Denise, Carl, Susan, and the Taylors all just had their homeowner's insurance canceled because of the wildfire risk."

"Yeah." He nods and cocks his head at me. "And there's the wildfire risk itself."

In spite of all that, the market value of this offbeat, not-to-code bungalow has more than doubled. It's coastal California, after all. The place would be desirable to the right people. It's a very sweet, very small house tucked into rugged hills near gorgeous deserted beaches on the California coast. You can walk to a good swimming and kayaking spot on a pretty-clean river. It's too far from San Francisco to be prime real estate and too modest to be a fancy vacation home. But there are moderate-sized towns nearby, so it's possible to have a job. The people are diverse and relaxed. And in Northern California, one does not lack for culture. The nearest town, eight miles away, has an excellent independent bookstore. A library is open four afternoons a week. You can get the Sunday *New York Times* at a hotel. Five coffee shops—not Starbucks—are within nine miles. Inscrutably, a Korean family operates a great sushi house. A movie theater in a Quonset hut shows one quality flick five nights a week year-round but has no heat in winter. They provide blankets in the lobby.

We love it here and want to stay. If you go inland, even just a few miles, the summer gets too hot. Like every other place in the whole world except this one, it is hot, getting hotter, and hotter yet. Our house has a reliably cool ocean breeze. It took all our fumbling lives to get here. It seems so wrong that we have to leave so soon. But the sale of the house is our ticket to a decent future. We are hoping to spend the profit enjoying our final years renting from someone else. But so far we haven't found that citadel of no responsibility.

And nothing compares to the best things about where we are, so we have no place we want to go.

Similarly, when we need to vacate the premises as people come to look at the house, there is no place we want to go for even short periods of time. The first time it happened, we took a walk on the road. The next time, we thought about getting in the car and going for a drive, but we didn't want to. So we walked into the neighbor's woods until we were out of sight of our house. This worked so well that we do it every time now. We can go in our pajamas. We take books to read and walking sticks for the steep slope, food and water, a camera and binoculars, and something to sit on. Sometimes our cat follows us. He rolls around in the exciting new dirt and sits on our laps as we read. We feel like a family and take pictures of him. Sitting out in the woods, we are not always sure when the people have come or if they have gone. One time we moved closer so we could watch, but my husband had worn his light blue shirt and white cap. Someone waved at us from our deck. We went farther into the woods and down the hill.

Having strangers go through your house has problems. One time people removed the gate from its hinges trying to get in. It seems obvious to us how to do it correctly, but after that, we put up a sign: *Latch*, with an arrow pointing to it. We put up other signs around the house, black felt tip on pink index cards. At the kitchen sink: *For filtered water, turn HANDLE, not spigot.* At the top of the inside stairway: *Light switch for stairs—steep.* At the top of the outside stairway: *Caution, steep stairs.*

The signs were boring. We made up better signs:

If you lived here, you'd be home by now.
If you lived here, you'd be drunk by now.
If you lived here, your own food would be on the walls.

Sauces do splash when you're cooking. We cleaned. We put up a handrail on some of the stairs.

We look at our options. There is a small trailer park, call it a mobile home park, right down the hill. It's on the river and has a good private beach. Amazingly, the lay of the land is such that most of it does not flood. But the homes are small and close together, and we hear it is a nasty little community of meddling people on shared septic. No washing machines are allowed; you must use their coin laundry only. Management seems to be in the hands of various residents, resulting in undecipherable, rigid disorganization. "And we'd still have a building to maintain," my husband reminds me. "Plus space rent."

Another trailer park is thirty minutes inland and, therefore, yes, in the heat. But the homes are bigger, and the people seem happier. It's in the country but close to a small town. That place is on my possible list. "But we'd still have to maintain it," my husband points out. "Plumbing and electrical can go wrong. The roof. The foundation. The whole mess." He's got a touch of PTSD from keeping our present house from exploding or sliding down the hill.

"But it would be a much smaller building," I counter. "With a tiny yard. We could find one in top condition."

"And a street four feet from the front door and a barking dog living next door."

He has a point. And it is so far from the ocean.

So hot.

Between our incomes and the money from the sale, we think we can afford to rent a house or duplex. In the right location, that could be perfect, though it would have the insecurity and lack of control that comes with being renters. But is our best option really to leave solid land behind and swim out into unknown waters, expecting to find a raft out there somewhere? A three-bedroom, two-bath raft with a garage, nice porches, and quiet nature all around. Safe. With the perfect landlord. And out of the heat.

Buyers continue to look at our house. We wonder who they are, these other people looking for their next raft. The time they spotted us, we also got a glimpse of them: a somewhat obese couple who we figure could never live with those stairs. But who are the others? We've found a place to sit where they can't see us but we can see them, with binoculars.

There is a young woman on her own, just the right size to live in a small, pretty house. *She may be the one*, I think. I imagine who she is: she wants to save money for retirement and live in a quiet place and will drive forty minutes to work in the bigger town. She can handle the steep stairs, and she loves the wide windows looking out on endless green outside. The broker, a rosy-cheeked man in his sixties, escorts her onto the deck. He turns away from her and tries to make a call on his cell phone, but of course there is no signal in these hills. He walks out the driveway, pushing buttons on his phone, vainly searching.

She looks out into the woods in our direction but doesn't see us. We are low to the ground, wearing camo and holding very still. The binoculars show delight on her face as she looks across the canyon through the majestic Douglas firs rooted in the slope far below, their trunks rising past the house to heights above. They have remained in their precarious rootedness for many decades and perhaps will remain for many more. Similarly huge trees are more or less rooted in the slope above the house and soar almost too far to see. She may not notice that both below and above, fallen giants have speared downhill some distance from the craters left by their house-sized, upturned roots or the jagged remains where they broke off.

But the next prospective buyers notice this. The man is big. He is looking up the hill at the trees that will flatten even his burly self when they fall. The wife, slimmer, is looking down the hill. She eyes the flimsy handrail on the steep stairway joining two decks and asks the broker, "Is that the only way to get down there?" *If you lived here, you would be dead by now.*

We made a list of the improvements we've made to the house over fifteen years, and it was good. *If you lived here, you'd be safe from the propane tank exploding next to your front door because we moved it. You'd be less wet when you entered the house on a rainy day because we put polyurethane sheets above the front entrance. You would not so often fall down the steep stairs outside because we put up a handrail, however flimsy.*

More couples come to look. There is a young pair, looking to buy their first home. They notice the wood plank floors that need to be refinished and the burn spot on the floor inside the cabinet below the sink, from the fire that started in the wastebasket one time. *If you lived here, you'd have a lot of work to do on the weekends.* She looks in the fridge. Closing the refrigerator door, she notes the scratches on it from the night a possum moseyed through the open front door and then desperately tried to escape my husband's efforts to capture it in a box.

Two gay men from the city are shopping for a weekend retreat. *If you lived here, you would have done landscaping by now.* They look behind the curtains that serve as our closet doors and notice too many clothes, including the same clothes usually strewn about on chairs but now stuffed in wads on the shelf.

A couple on vacation from Nebraska fell in love with the area yesterday, and today they are house-dreaming before they go home. He thinks: *if I lived here, my in-laws would never visit.* He is charmed by the idea of having a woodstove. But seeing the large piles of harvested and scavenged firewood, he wonders if the electric wall heater really warms the place enough. (It doesn't. *If you lived here, you'd be cutting wood, shoveling ashes, cleaning the chimney, and you would still be cold on winter mornings.*) She whispers to him: *for this price, we can get four bedrooms, three acres, and a pool outside Omaha.*

All options are still open for us. I've put us on a seven-year waiting list for rent-supported senior housing in the city, twenty-five miles directly east into the heat. Could we live in the heat? Could we live in a one-bedroom apartment? We don't want to. What if it was a travel trailer and we could move around the country? We don't want to move around; we like it here. We don't want to join the friendly cast of characters in *Nomadland*.

I search the internet for the perfect rental. I find several, but they are all perfectly beyond our price range. A house on the coast would be most perfect, but they are rare, and even a small one rents for four thousand a month. I find options we could afford inland but with neighbors too close, bright streetlights outside, Safeway delivery trucks idling in the alley behind. Also, being inland, they are in the you-know-what.

"Don't find one yet!" my husband yells. "We're not ready!" He has been going through his boxes of nuts, bolts, screws, nails, hinges, springs, and miscellaneous metal parts salvaged from equipment he used for many years until he could no longer fix it and finally dismantled it. Those mystery parts he often uses to repair something else. He shakes a densely packed baggie and says proudly, "Two or three pounds going to the thrift shop." He holds up another baggie. "Another four pounds into the recycle." He calls this packing. But the garage and sheds are still full of tools, as are the shelves and tables in the workshop. "I still use them. And who knows what we'll need at our next place?" Two kayaks sit under tarps below a wall. We can no longer get them up on top of the car, but maybe we'll move to a place on the water.

I'm supposed to be decluttering too. Shall I give my Turkish carpets to nieces and nephews who don't want them? Wherever we go, can't they cover the floors and hang on the walls? Artwork also covers the walls, with more stashed under the bed. How can we get rid of our excess of vases when we fill them up with flowers and greenery from outside every day? Books? Some of them can go, and they do, in a box or bag to the library book sale every few months. Papers? That's another story. Which is exactly what they are, and my three unfinished novels are not yet expendable.

We're in the woods. A couple comes to see the place. They seem middle-aged or older, but we can't really tell. One of them, a woman, is tall and blonde; the man, or maybe another woman, is shorter and stocky and is the one taking charge, gesturing here and there with the taller one nodding. If they are old, the steep stairs are not a good feature. Still, they are a lively pair and certainly not as old as us. The stocky one has muscular calves and might ride a bicycle, which is hard in these hills, but people do it. The tall one probably likes to take long walks, and hills are good for cardio.

Stocky has a vision: *If we lived here, we could replace the old decks and add a small room off the north side, for a guest bedroom and more storage. We could move the washer and dryer from where they sit outside on the top deck and put them down below and build a proper rain shelter over them.*

Tall one agrees and embellishes: *If we lived here, we could grow tomatoes in pots, like these people have done: small red and yellow globes nestled among big leaves. That cute little studio building with all the windows and skylights could be a playroom for Josh when he comes and a sewing room the rest of the time. I could spread out my quilting materials and have good light to work. I could play classical music on the radio and not bother you.*

They giggle with excitement and do a high five before strolling down the driveway. The tall one is walking in a certain way—is she pregnant? Maybe she's not as old as I thought.

I wake in the night to the beauty of silence and the sub-dued whinnying of two screech owls. Within moments, my heart is tight and thoughts racing: *No! I don't want to go.* I turn over onto my side and cover my head with the blanket, heart still tight. *We will NEVER find a place as good as this. We will NEVER find a place!* I get up and climb the narrow stairs to the kitchen and eat peanut butter and drink almond milk. My heart calms down. The owls have moved on, and in the blanket of silence my panic is slowly replaced by immense gratitude. And sadness.

We're in the woods again. There is a single man walking across the deck. Now he is peering over the rail at the fallen trees with their ancient bark crumbling off, the mess of ferns dying from the drought. He looks out at the view of trees, treetops, all across the canyon. He sees no other houses, hears road noise far in the distance, hears jays and chickadees close by. He looks up at blue sky and soft drifting clouds and sees the hawk's nest that will be occupied again next spring. *If I lived here, the night would be dark and quiet. The full moon would come up there in the east, a huge golden globe rising through the trees and shining into the house most of the night, circling through all the wide windows. I could take walks down to the river, drive easily to the ocean. Build fires in the woodstove and heat food in a pan on top. If I lived here, I could go out into those woods and sit for a while, read a book.* The man walks to the front of the house, disappearing from our sight.

Summer is fading when Tall and Stocky return for another look, without their broker. They just turn up at the gate. They're both women—Dylan (the stocky one) and Jaymia. At close quarters, I see that she *is* pregnant. We all smile and talk outside the front door.

They want to know about the water stain they noticed on the bedroom ceiling, and we confess the roof leaked once but we painted the shingles to seal the cracks. "Has it rained since then?" Dylan asks.

My husband is quick to reply. "I used exterior deck paint. It pretty much works."

Dylan looks at him, the question unanswered.

"No," I say. "It hasn't rained since."

Dylan nods. "Thanks."

We escort them down the driveway, my husband walking with Dylan, Jaymia and me lagging behind. "We've lived here fifteen years, and we're getting too old to really keep it up," I explain.

"It's a sweet little house. Dylan's a contractor, so it 's important to her to get an accurate picture of what she would need to fix. But she can take care of whatever it needs." She lingers. "We've been together twenty years, and we're downsizing. Which is silly now!" She pats her belly. She stops to look back at the house. "The privacy of this place is unusual. We really want a private place."

"Yeah, we really like how private it is. Sometimes you hear the neighbor down the hill if she's on the phone out on the deck," I tell her. Jaymia is easy to talk to. "It's hard to leave. We really love it."

"We love it too!" she says. Then, with a bit more reserve: "We'll see."

It's August. We still have no place to go, and time is getting short. When the rains come in the fall, it's all over for selling a house. We don't even pretend to pack anymore and don't keep the place all that clean. I continue to search the internet, and my husband continues to say that's a waste of time because we can't move if we can't sell, and we can't sell if we can't move.

I've started singing a song in what I hope is an incantation:

"Dylan and Jaymia, if it's all the same to ya, why not buy the house you love?

Dylan and Jaymia, no one will blame ya if you buy the house you love."

Coming out of the shower one night, I hear my husband picking up the tune:

"Dylan and Jaymia, life's just a game-i-ya, come out and play-mi-ya,

Better buy the house you love!"

There is a nibble. The single woman who admired the big trees returns, with her broker, to look at the house again. She wants the house but is afraid she might need someone to help with the upkeep. She crosses paths with the single man, who parked down the road and is furtively walking around to get another look. He likes the place but is thinking he might be pretty lonely up here by himself. They talk, admiring the house together. Soon they are admiring each other.

Meantime, Dylan and Jaymia have heard our song.

167

They are eager to move into their downsized nest. There are hints that an offer might come before the rains do. If, in fact, there are to be any rains this year.

Still no place for us to go, but we continue to act like the house might yet sell. We've rented a storage unit and mapped out a vacation route up the coast for October and November. We'll arrange long-term stays in motels from which we can continue our online search for perfection and return quickly to this area, our beloved home part of the world, to look at a place and put down a deposit. I've done the math, something I'm not good at, and found that we can afford a safe, spacious, private, quiet, comfortable rental in a wonderful location. We'll spend down our profits from selling the house, and that will give us sixteen years worth of rental. Will we care if we are penniless when we are in our mid-nineties?

We'll leave, but we're coming back. We're on our way to a raft, and we hope to find a better raft. We're letting go of the shore to swim through waves of uncertainty, unsettled and conflicting opinions, the grief of a major loss, the thinly covered terror of all aging people, and the ever-hotter reality of the world. Maui is on fire. We realize that this whole life is just a raft.

It's Labor Day when the break comes: the newly paired singles are in a modest bidding war with Dylan and Jaymia. We think the younger folks deserve an easier start. *If you lived here, you'd be divorced by now.* Also, their offer may be a little fragile since they just met.

So we choose the downsizers, who are ready to pay cash. We guess they've been through enough in life to handle this home. We accept their generous offer, and everybody is seriously beginning to pack. It is really terribly sad for us. But we can truthfully say this to them: *if you lived here, you'd be happy by now.*

ACKNOWLEDGMENTS

So much help from so many. It's nonsense to thank only some of them, but here they are:

For showing me the possibility of pursuing dreams, thank you to my father, Howard Day.

For steadfast encouragement, patience, and an open heart, thank you to my sister, Joan Johnson.

For long-ago encouragement, thanks to Candy Clayton and the English teacher at Mizzou.

For support in the not-quite-so-long ago, thanks to Guy Biederman, Vic and Sara Campbell, and the Napa writers group including Arlene Bernstein, Julie van der Ryn, and Diana Morley.

For help and inspiration these days, thank you to Jo-Anne Rosen, Marko Fong, Linda Saldaña, Richard Gustafson,

Nick Valdez, Sarah Amador, and Amanda Yskamp.

For friendship and encouraging my writing over fifty years, thanks to Barry Leibman and Maria Monroe.

For friendship and encouraging my writing over twenty-five years, thanks to Helen Cooluris, Catherine Sharp, and Nell Kneibler.

Thanks to editors: my first editor, Kim Lim, for her lighthearted discernment and encouragement; Sydney Weinberg, for being instructive and appreciative of my efforts to learn; and especially to Margaret Diehl, for her clearsighted understanding and esteem of my work.

Thanks to Asya Blue for terrific book design. Thanks to Ellen Tarlin for sensitive proofreading.

For the inspiration and delight they provide, thanks to all the writers I love.

For unseen but enduring help given, I thank my four twosomes as well as the many others of whom I am aware and unaware.

And in his own impossible-to-categorize category, thanks to Doug, for the everything he gives me.

Different versions of the following stories were published as follows:

"The Sundown Side of the Rock" was published in *Canyon Voices*, Issue 10, Fall 2014, www.canyonvoices.asu.edu.

"Royal Flush" was published in the Spring 2015 issue of *Persimmon Tree*, www.persimmontree.org.

"Stupid Buddha" was published in the April/May 2015 issue of *The Otter*, www.ottermagazine.com.

"If You Lived Here" was published in Issue No. 13, September 2016 of *Buffalo Almanack*, and won that issue's Inkslinger Award.

"Crystal Monkey" was published in 2023 in Vol. 44, Issue 1 & 2 of *Pilgrimage*, www.pilgrimagepress.org. Published by Colorado State University, Pueblo.

ABOUT THE AUTHOR

Judith Day is the author of *Glowing in the Dark, Stories of Wounded Healers*. She has been a cook and a cab driver, and she has graduate degrees in history and psychology. Since 1990 she has worked in private practice as a psychotherapist. She has also worked in emergency psychiatric response, inpatient psychiatric settings, residential treatment, low-fee mental health clinics, and as a military family life consultant. She has taught mindfulness meditation since 1993.

Married for forty years, Judith lives with her husband near the ocean in northern California. She may be contacted at books@judithday.com.